THE LONG RIDERS

Up in the Wyoming Territory, Broadbaker saw a chance to pick up eight hundred head of cattle for the price of a .45 slug, and he took it. But he didn't reckon with the power of hate in a man who's been shot in the back and left for dead — and he didn't reckon on his victim having a couple of partners willing to ride a thousand miles to kill a man they'd never met.

DAN CUSHMAN

THE LONG RIDERS

Complete and Unabridged

LINFORD
Leicester

First published in the
United States of America

First Linford Edition
published April 1995

Copyright © 1967 by Fawcett Publications, Inc

British Library CIP Data

Cushman, Dan
  The long riders.—Large print ed.—
  Linford western library
  I. Title II. Series
  813.54 [F]

  ISBN 0–7089–7697–2

Published by
F. A. Thorpe (Publishing) Ltd.
Anstey, Leicestershire

Set by Words & Graphics Ltd.
Anstey, Leicestershire
Printed and bound in Great Britain by
T. J. Press (Padstow) Ltd., Padstow, Cornwall

This book is printed on acid-free paper

1

Man in Hiding

THE road entered Lodgepole, Wyoming Territory, from the east. It was the old Overland road from Fort Russell, and the town, once an important stage station, had fallen into hard times, having been bypassed by the Union Pacific Railroad five miles to the south.

"There it is, the queen city of the Lamotte country," said Leo Glass, pulling in for a good look at it. He was lean and tall with good shoulders. His mother, who still lived in St. Joseph, Missouri, had named him Lionel, but the kids around town had nicknamed him 'Leo the Lion.' It ended by being Leo. Leo the Lion seemed to fit him not at all. He was an easy man to get on with. He had never started trouble in his life, but he had finished some that had been started by others. The man with him went by the name of Old Dad. He was about forty-five years old. It was a young man's country.

"I can't say it looks very queenly to me," said Dad.

"What are you talking about? Put a few buildings in here and there, and it'd look like Denver."

"I hope they got some ice, I've just been priming myself for a bottle of lager off from ice."

The town was perfectly quiet. Scarcely a horsefly was moving. They rode up to the hotel. Their arrival had caused no excitement. It was very hot. It was too hot for anyone to move.

"'The Overland Hotel,'" Dad read slowly. "Is this where he's staying?"

"It's the only hotel in town."

"Are you going right in and ask for him?"

"Any reason I shouldn't?"

"You know him better than I do. Him and his reputation. You know how peculiar the letter sounded — all about keeping this quiet and that mum and something else under your hat. I thought maybe the marshals were after him."

"Oh, hell, Dad, he'd have said so. The Kid isn't so bad. All that Panhandle stuff is a long way behind him."

They dismounted. There was a horse trough made of a hollowed cottonwood. It had been so long in use that green water moss had grown in the bottom. The water looked fresh and cool. The horses drank, and it was a temptation to get right in and drink with them.

"I'd sure fondle a beer," said Dad.

The word BAR had been painted ornately on the big window. The masterpiece of some itinerant sign painter, it managed to incorporate a waterfall, snow-capped mountains, and bunches of grapes all in the design. It had faded like everything else. Dirty playing cards were scattered over the plank sidewalk.

"Ain't you going to take your gun?" Dad asked.

Leo's gun and belt were on the saddle horn, where he had hung them for comfort. "No. If I go back for it now, it might look unfriendly. I'm the friendliest man alive. Or it might look like I was afraid they'd steal it. I wouldn't want to ride in and imply the folks were thieves."

"Well, it's your property."

"I'll let you shoot it out for me, Dad."

"I could kill 'em with spit. This stuff I been hawking is like bullets."

They passed through a hot, empty lobby and an arch into the bar. The bartender got his foot down from the sink and walked over to say hello. The beer was in a tub of water with wet burlap over it. It was cool and mild.

"I was in hopes you'd have ice," said Dad

"Come back in January," the bartender said mildly.

"I'll bet it's cold here in January."

4

"We had it forty-six below. The wells all froze. We had to haul ice from Lamotte Creek and thaw it."

"You know a fellow named Frank Maybee? They call him Kid Maybee."

"I know him. I haven't seen him. Not for a couple of weeks. He was up here scouting for a trail herd."

"You don't know where he went?"

"No, he didn't say."

He was a better-than-average liar . . .

* * *

"You see?" said Dad when they were leaving. "We had the ride for nothing. He wrote you that hurry-up-get-rich letter and then never even stuck around."

"He's here all right."

"What makes you think so?"

"I don't know. Just a flash I got of that bartender in the mirror when I asked. He probably thinks we're bounty hunters."

"Who'd take you for a bounty

5

hunter? You haven't even got a gun."

"You look like a bounty hunter. Maybe a detective that Wells Fargo would send out. That cold killer look in your eye."

There was still nobody in the lobby, but a weighted drape was swinging to rest behind the desk, although at that hour there was not a stir of breeze in all windy Wyoming.

"You see? The bartender came in here. He waited for us to get out of sight back of that stained glass partition and slipped around the back way. Now we'll call the clerk, and he'll say the Kid isn't here. This is almighty strange. He's hiding out all right."

They went to the counter and rang a little bell. After a minute there was a footstep, and a woman came in. She was about thirty-five years old and had an aristocratic bearing.

"You got a Mr. Maybee here? I'm a friend."

"Maybee — like maybe?"

"It's capital M, and a double E. He

wrote me he'd be here."

"What's your name?"

"Glass. Leo Glass."

He went through his pockets and found the Kid's letter, sweat-curled from carrying and addressed to him in Cheyenne.

"Leave your gun here," she said to Dad. "It will be all right under the counter when you get back."

"I'd just as soon stay here with it."

"Do what the lady says and come along," said Glass. "You got to excuse him, ma'am. His mother was scared by the Mexican war."

"It was lots previous to that," Dad said, taking off his gun, an old conversion .44, and putting it away with the belt wrapped around it.

She took them up some narrow stairs and down a hallway. She stopped at a closed door and listened.

"Fred?"

"Yah?" a man answered, and a bed squeaked.

"It's Leo Glass. He has somebody with him."

"Who's with him?"

"It's all right, Kid," said Leo. "It's Dad Haze."

"Come on in."

The woman unlocked the door. Kid Maybee, an angular, long-jawed man, lay in bed with his knees sticking up and a six-shooter making a saddle of the covers between them. After seeing who it was and exchanging glances with the woman, he put the gun on the floor and said, "Thanks, Emma. I'll talk to 'em alone."

She left, closing the door behind her.

2

Kid Maybee's Story

"WHAT'S the trouble, Kid?" asked Glass with genuine concern. He had never particularly liked Maybee, but he hadn't disliked him, either. Half the stories about him probably weren't true. He had come from a pretty rough area down in the Panhandle. It was a no-man's-land without state jurisdiction, no law of any kind, so all he'd done, Glass imagined, were the things necessary to stay alive. Anyhow, dredging all that up would seem to be raking unfair advantage now, because Maybee, the Kid, was obviously a sick man.

"I'm feeling better now. The Doc came over special from Medicine Bow. It cost me fifty dollars, carfare and all, but it was worth it. I was all mashed up inside. You see, we had this roan horse — I'd never ridden him before — and the damn wrangler had put a curb bit on him, and I was no sooner in the saddle than *whang*! He put me right over his head into the side of a wagon and then he rolled over on me. I thought I'd be all right in a couple of days, but I kept bleeding internally, so they hauled me down here in a wagon. The Doc couldn't be sure without operating and he didn't want to do that, but he thought I had a ruptured intestine. He bound me all up and gave me some medicine. I can get up and out of bed a little now, but I won't be able to ride for three or four months. He said the main danger now was pneumonia of the bowels."

"You stay right in bed. I'm glad you wrote."

There were peculiar brown marks across his face, particularly his cheekbone and forehead on the left side. He had lost some teeth, too. It might have been where the horse slammed him, but it looked more as if he had taken a beating from someone's fists and the blue bruises had got to the yellow stage. There was a bandage around his middle. He had revealed it when tossing the covers back from the heat, but it was not so tight as the kind used for binding a man down, it seemed, and there was a pad underneath and an opening to admit a little hollow reed for a wound that was suppurating. But that didn't mean he had to be bullet-wounded. He might have been punctured by anything. Strange, however, he hadn't mentioned it.

"There's likely to be a lot of money in this, just like I wrote you," said Maybee, getting a folder and some papers from beside his bed. "How the two of you want to split it is your own affair. I'll give you half and I'll keep half. These are the papers for four hundred head of longhorns of the Hammerhead brand I own outright.

These tallied out four twenty-one when we drove from Colorado. Then I have a forty percent interest in three hundred eighty more, branded KY, Seventy-Seven and J-Bar-J. The transfers and conditional bills are all here — signed, everything. Your share of these will be half my forty, or twenty. That makes eight hundred head all told. You owe two thousand dollars to me. That's half of what I had to pay for the ones I own. The Hammerheads. Ten dollars a head."

"Where would I get two thousand dollars? I never had that much in my life. I had an uncle that did, but he went to jail."

"That's all right. I don't need it now. You can owe me. You can *owe* that much, can't you?"

"Yes, I can owe money with the best of 'em."

"All right, it's owed. We can just subtract that from the total when you sell."

"Sell where? I don't understand this."

12

"When you sell to the only market there is in those parts — north in the gold camps of Montana. Do you know what they're paying for trail-run cattle up there? Forty-five dollars a head! They paid that for the McMillan herd. I saw it on the telegraph. It'll be higher now."

Dad cried, "You're asking us to drive across Cheyenne country."

"I'm *suggesting* you make a pack of money for yourselves. You might net twelve thousand dollars in two or three months. A man can take some risk for that."

"It figures at about ten thousand — minus losses and expenses," said Glass.

"Suicide!" said Dad.

"If you want a good, safe job, try clerking in a store. Anyhow, you'll have the wagon families along."

"What wagon families? Who are they?"

"They're some settlers that sort of follow along for protection. You can

13

talk it over with them when you get there. If you're worried about Cheyennes, you could set off to the north with quite a little army."

"How big a crew you got? I haven't the money to pay them. And where is this herd, anyway?"

"I was going to tell you about all that. I threw in with Broadbaker's outfit. He's moving up from Nebraska — "

"Andy Broadbaker, the man-eater?"

"He might take a shot at you for homesteading his range, but he's not a bad one to have along if the Indians attack."

"You mean Broadbaker's driving his whole outfit to Montana?"

"No, he's going to the Popo Agie. Him and the pilgrims unless they change their minds. And the Arbogasts."

"Judge Arbogast's old outfit?"

"The same. They're all moving north and they're moving west. That south country has gone to hell. You can raise a hundred pounds of beef on the grass up here while those southern cattle are putting on twenty pounds of whang leather and bone. Don't tell Broadbaker what your plans are when it's time for you to turn north, just cut loose. The emigrant wagons may one or two decide to stay with Broadbaker, but he's such a catamount I doubt it. They'll have a gutful of him without going to the Popo country. You may need a guide, but you can pick one up in Casper or one of those camps along the old Oregon road. At all events, those wagoners will give you numbers. About thirty guns in case of Indians — and of course any more you can pick up on the trail. You're sort of obliged to let 'em eat on our beef. Just watch the drag for the critters most likely to go down and butcher them. They're just as good in a stew, and their meat will keep better. It will be turned to jerky by the time you skin it."

"Why'd he try to kill you?" Glass asked, turning on him suddenly.

"Who try to kill me? Nobody tried to kill me! A horse rolled on me."

"All right, Kid."

"What the hell are all these questions? If you don't want to go out and make yourself nine thousand dollars, a fortune, the only real hunk of money you ever got hold of in your whole two-bit — "

"I said all right."

Maybee handed him a paper. "You're supposed to sign this," he said, weakened and lying back to rest.

"What is it?"

"I had a suitcase lawyer draw it up. It tallies all the cattle, and you got to take my word. It might be off fifteen critters but no more. Then there's fifteen saddle horses, some gear, a wagon and two good teams. There's a big German kid driving for me, just working his passage. I just wish you'd keep hold of my saddle and bridle. They were made special for me in St. Louis. If it was only you and me, I'd not ask you to sign a thing. But I got a mother down in Arkansas, and if anything should happen to me — you know, if I got to bleeding again — I want her to be provided for."

"I'll sign. Have you got a pencil?"

"Use a bullet. Bullet lead leaves a mark more permanent than ink. Legal, absolutely. Reminds you not to welsh on a deal. But of course I know you wouldn't. You're a stubborn one, but you're honest. And you're one hell of a good man with cattle."

"Thanks," said Glass. There were some .44 caliber bullets on the dresser. He took one and signed. It was sure as hell a permanent signature. You had to press down so hard that the lead became part of the paper.

"There's something else I ought to tell you," said the Kid.

"What's that?"

"Billy Grand is working for Broadbaker. Scout."

"Scout? You mean hired gunman."

"Broad calls him a scout."

3

A Taste of Blood

IT took all the money they had for two packhorses amd the list of supplies Kid Maybee had enumerated. They set out at dawn and rode northwestward over some flanks of the Laramies and camped among the pines. Next morning they came out on some wide bench country and looked across at the valleys of the Bow and the Little Crooked and beyond to the million square miles, more or less, cut by the bird-track patterns of other drainages and by the east-west dip of the Platte.

"According to Maybee, that herd was on Buffalo Creek when he got hurt," said Leo Glass. "That was ten days ago, and they must have covered considerable ground, even making the big swing up and around to miss the mountains. If we turn to north-northeast, we ought to cut their trail about tomorrow."

Long before cutting the trail they saw their dust. It had been dry, and the white clay made a slowly drifting haze that was visible for a hundred miles. Yes, a hundred miles in that clear atmosphere. Then at sunset they crested a last plateaulike slab of the country and looked down on the herd itself.

It had been driven down to a creek that here and there spread out to form cattail sloughs. The bottoms were as much as a mile in width, and the herd would be bedded down in bunches for a considerable distance. It would take a large crew to tend a herd bedded down in that manner. Along the near side, away from the dustdrift that still hung over the cattle, were a couple of wagon camps. One probably belonged to Broadbaker's outfit and the Arbogasts, and the other to the pilgrims — those wagon families that had no real tie-up with him but were just stringing along for the protection. He could see the flash of women's dresses, the shimmering look of calico at sundown. The wagons of both camps had been drawn up in crude circles, although the Indians were not being troublesome — Cheyennes far to the north and Sioux in the Black Hills with an army watching them.

"That's a big herd," Glass remarked. "That's far and away the biggest herd that ever came this far north."

"And a dry season to find water for 'em," said Dad.

They still had half an hour's ride. The ground descended in gentle steps. Wolves kept appearing singly just beyond rifle range, following the herd for fallen ones or awaiting the gut and head leavings of the butcher crews. The voices of men could be heard. Riders were at work pulling rope-mired cattle out of the shallows. A beef, fresh-killed and cooling, hung on a cottonwood limb near a cookwagon. In the last ray of sun they could see the flies rising and falling over it like a mist of bronze. They could smell smoke and the herd odors of oily hair and trampled dirt and droppings, and their horses were encouraged by the downhill and the smell of water.

The last descent was through slots in cutbanks, loose dirt, and chokecherry brush. They stopped to water at a scummy backslough so close to camp that scraps of conversation could be heard.

"Oh, hello," a cowboy said when they came on through bushes and cottonwoods. He did not at first realize they were strangers. The fact came to him only when he saw the packhorses. "Say, you might have got shot coming up like that from the blind side. The Indians tried to run off a dozen saddle horses yesterday. You headed for Casper?"

"We're looking for the Broadbaker-Arbogast herd. And Maybee's."

"This is it. But if you're looking for Kid Maybee, you're aways late. He got killed on the other side of the Laramies."

"How'd it happen?" Glass asked, stopping Dad with a glance.

"I wasn't even there at the time." He didn't want to discuss it, but he was friendly. "That's the cookwagon, the one with the red flag."

"What does the flag mean?"

"It means, 'Keep off, you hungry varmints, till supper's ready.'"

They dismounted and walked, getting the stiffness of riding out of their muscles. It was settling twilight in the bottoms, and the flames of the cookfire looked bright. Men were gathering for supper but keeping twenty or thirty yards distance. The cook was a tall, spare man and he had two helpers. Both helpers kept on the run, but the cook took his own good time. The smells were tantalizing.

"Visitors," called the cowboy.

They caused some excitement.

Everyone wanted to know if they had been in a town with a telegraph. They wanted the results of the Mace-O'Connell fight in New Orleans for the heavyweight championship of the world. It had gone to Mace when his American opponent failed to come up for the gong in the 58th round. There were cries of disappointment and one of triumph. One man seemed to be collecting all the bets. He was young and very good-looking, with a shock of unruly blond hair and an expensive hat, sitting at an angle on his head. He was Billy Grand, the 'scout' mentioned by Maybee.

"I'm giving you a silver dollar for bringing the news!" he said. "A full day's pay for a working man."

"I'm one of the owners here. I couldn't take it."

"They were looking for Kid Maybee," someone said.

Grand kept smiling, but there was a difference. He had a pair of very cold eyes. "You're a little late."

"So we hear."

"Well, that's how it is — some win and some lose, some live and some don't, some get rich and some get poor. That's the way the cards are stacked."

"Stacked?"

"It's how they fall. Real sorry you have to bring good news and get bad. You friends of the Kid's?"

"Yes. I'm Leo Glass. This is Daddy Haze."

"I'm Billy Grand."

"I know."

"You do?" He was pleased.

"He saw your picture up in the Wells Fargo office, Billy," somebody said.

"No, I saw you in person down in Wichita." Leo did not add that he had seen him kill a man in Wichita. He killed a man, surrendered his gun, stood hearing, and was freed, all in an hour.

"Say, I've had some great times in Wichita."

"Is Andy Broadbaker around?"

"His wagon — yonder."

It was a small but solid wagon with a tight canvas top and a real door at the back. It sat somewhat removed, and there were other wagons and a tent farther on. As they watched, the door opened, and a man came down, using some steps.

He was tall and had to bend considerably to get under the door. He was wide through the shoulders, causing him to come rather sidewise. There was a heavy grace in all his movements. He had a head-up manner of a bull elk coming down the mountain. He had to be at least forty years old because he had been a big man down in Texas before the war. Later he had moved to Nebraska, cow, wheel, and kettle, and had occupied land along the Republican River, where he had become known as the man-eater. It was the story that he warned two settlers against taking up some favored springwater pasture under the new Homestead Act, and when they defied him, he killed them, tossed them in their burning shack, and had a bite from one of their roasted bodies. It was true enough he had killed them or had had them killed — Glass never heard that he had denied it — and he had burned them, because their blackened, mummylike bodies had been hauled up to North Platte City and displayed in an undertaking parlor, but the eating of roasted flesh was pure lie. It couldn't have been true because the marshals had dug their bodies out of the ashes. Anyway, it had caused quite an outcry. Both men had been Union veterans, and Broadbaker hailed from the South. It even reached the floor of Congress. The Stockman's Association saved him, reluctantly, but they did not like him. They made an outcast of him and no doubt provided one reason for his decision to move north.

"Hey, Broad," said the cook, "here's a couple fellows to see you."

Broadbaker walked over to shake hands. Firelight, striking the long way across his face, brought out its strong lines, the jaw, the cheekbones, the heavy bone above the eyes. His skin was the hue of oak leather. His eyes were small from years of sun. They were slits of blue.

"Leo Glass? Yes, I've heard of you." He shook hands with both of them. Then he waited, and his manner told them to be straight and brief.

"We're here to take over Kid Maybee's herd."

If Broadbaker had received a blow in the face, his reaction would not have been much different. He stopped himself with an obvious effort, and his hands opened and closed. The firelight lay on the knotted muscles of his jaw.

"What are you talking about?"

"The cattle. Kid Maybee said he had four hundred of his own and about that many on shares from down in Colorado. I have the papers. The brands are all here — and the tallies."

"Who gave you the papers?"

"He did."

"*Maybee* gave you the papers?"

"Yes, he did." Glass was straight about it but mild. There was something very wrong, but he wanted no trouble. He saw a girl ride in — she seemed to be about fifteen — and get down beyond Broadbaker's wagon and stand watching. It made him feel better because she must be one of the Arbogast family, and the Arbogasts had been big people in the Association.

"When did all this take place?" Broadbaker asked.

"Day before yesterday."

"I don't know what you're trying to do, Glass. If somebody sold you these cattle telling you he was Maybee — "

"I've known Kid Maybee for years."

"Then you'll be interested to know that he's dead."

"No, sir. He isn't."

Broadbaker wheeled and hit him. It was a movement of exasperation. He had given in to an uncontrollable impulse. The blow was so sudden that Leo Glass could not lift his hands. He could only flinch. And it crashed like an explosion, jarring every bone and joint in his body, and the next he knew he was on the ground, on his back, resting on his elbows, and Broadbaker stood over him.

He saw Dad backing and reaching for his gun. "No, Dad!" he cried. Grand would have killed him.

"What the hell?" yelled Dad in an outrage. "Why'd you do that?" he asked Broadbaker.

Glass did not try to get up. His jaw and head felt paralyzed. He might have thought he had no jaw at all except for touching it with his hand. Broadbaker, with his hands on his hips and his legs spread, waited for him to get up — probably to knock him down again. Glass got to his feet. He did it with a step in retreat. His lips were mashed, and he could taste blood. He looked around for his hat. There were broken bits of grass stuck to it. He brushed it off and put it on. Broadbaker still stood with his hands on his hips. Glass measured him and thought he could seem to stagger a step and then make the same maneuver that the big fellow himself had used — wheel, set, and smash. But there was an old poem: *Aces are up, And Deuces are down. Never start trouble, In the other man's town*. It just happened to flash in his mind.

"Well, this is your camp, Broadbaker. Your camp and your hospitality."

"You called me a liar."

"No, I didn't call you a liar. You said he was dead. But I talked to him alive day before yesterday afternoon. He was in bed, and the doctor had seen him. He had some inside bleeding, but he's going to get all right. I imagined all you fellows would be relieved to hear that. I imagined you'd be glad to know that we were here to do our part and take care of his property. It's half our property now. We bought it right down the middle."

Broadbaker had bruised his knuckles. He half smiled and examined them. "I suppose you have some documentary proof. You said something about it."

"Yes, I have."

"All right."

"It's kind of dark. Maybe we could go up to your wagon."

"There's light enough."

He was afraid Broadbaker would toss them in the fire. But he got them from his saddlebag.

"Here's our agreement, inventory, and so on. A lawyer drew it up, and of course there's copies."

Without glancing at a word on the papers, Broadbaker tore them down the middle. However, he did not deign to toss them into the fire. It was an act, not of destruction, but of contempt. He dropped them and trod on them.

"I could hang you for this — coming here and trying to assume a dead man's property. That's as bad as cattle stealing. I'd be perfectly within my rights if I tossed a rope over that limb and swung the both of you."

"And burn us afterward?" He thought Broadbaker would come for him again, but it was a thing he had to say. "And then what, Broadbaker? Would you move out of Wyoming like you moved out of Nebraska because nobody could stomach you? But where to? That's getting to be a problem. You can see the mountains off there — the Rockies. By the gods, Broadbaker, you've just about run out of country." He picked up the documents.

"That took quite a bit of guts," said Broadbaker.

Glass made no answer. He stood fitting the torn halves of pages together.

"What do you intend to do now?"

"There's only one thing I can do — go back and talk to the Kid. I'm in favor of seeing a lawyer, but he owns half, and I'll have to consult him. Nobody but a damn fool can say what will happen when he gets in court, but I think we have cause for judgment. It'll take some time. It may take years, but one day when you come down to the railroad with your cattle, there we'll be. I suppose we'll have writs and marshals and God-knows-what-all, and then you'll have to prove your position — that you couldn't turn over the Kid's property because he was dead. Which may be hard to prove if he's standing there beside me."

With that he turned away and might have ridden from camp, but a whip cut the grass and dirt near his boot toes, and a girl said, "Wait! Stop where you are."

4

The Girl with the Whip

HE looked at her. It was the girl he had seen earlier — the Arbogast girl. She had the true, imperious Arbogast features. He could remember her father, uncles, and older brothers when they came into St. Joseph, where his father was a freight contractor. A wild crowd, dressed in the finest, too much money to spend. Old Judge Arbogast had been the delegate to Congress in Washington, D.C., and once one of the richest men in the territory. The girl was slim and drawn up so tight in a riding skirt that he wondered how she could breathe. Her fury added to the effect. She was older than he first thought, but not a great deal. She drew back the whip — actually a long, braided quirt — and he thought for an instant she intended to lash him, across the face.

"Polly!" said Broadbaker.

"Why do you stand and listen to it? Why?"

"I don't want trouble."

She looked at Glass from toes to head, and her lips turned with contempt. "You're lower than a snake. You knew this man left Nebraska partly to escape those lies. He should hang you on that tree, but you know he won't because of the stories they'd tell. You even stood there and named him man-burner and man-eater! That didn't take nerve. That was a coward's thing to do. But you won't go to a lawyer. Or a court or a judge. You'll leave here and tell it around that Kid Maybee was murdered. You came here to extort money or cattle. And not getting what you came for, you'll go away and tell the lie."

"If you're convinced of that, miss — "

"Yes, Maybee was killed in this camp. Or near it. But Broad didn't

35

do it. They fought, and it was a fair fight. He fought with him like a man, in the open. But your Kid Maybee didn't take his beating like a man. Tell him about the ambush, Billy." She motioned to Billy Grand. "Come on, tell him how he really got killed."

"Well, I was asleep. But something — I think the horses — yes, it was the horses woke me up. It was late, and Broad had been someplace. He was just coming back to the wagon. I guess he'd been over at Lonnie's. Anyhow, I happened to see this gunshine. It was the Kid, like I said. I yelled and made him miss. Then we had a run through the night. I happened to get in a lucky shot. That was about all."

"Would you like to see his grave?" asked Polly Arbogast.

"Did *you* see it?" asked Glass.

"It's back there!"

"Did you see it?"

She wouldn't answer him. She

indicated it was of small importance whether she'd actually seen it or not.

"Did you see his body?"

"Oh, the hell with you!" she cried.

"Who did see his body?" Did *you* see it, Broad?"

"No," he admitted.

"You don't put any stock in this, do you?" she cried. "Andy, you don't actually believe — "

"Ask the wagon bunch," said Grand, motioning in the direction of the other camp. "They sure got no love for us. I think they'd pull out and leave if they weren't afraid of the Indians. Go up there and ask Denison. One of 'em is a preacher. His name is Brown. He buried him. You'll believe a preacher, won't you?"

"That's right," the girl said, to Glass. "Those pilgrims owe nothing to us. At least they *think* they don't. They're just stringing along for protection with an idea of taking up land someplace. They'd shake us in a minute if they didn't need our protection." She turned in exasperation and addressed Broadbaker. "Lies and accusations! Is it just going to go on and on and on? Their lies drove you out of Nebraska and now they're following you across Wyoming! How long do you have to put up with it?"

"It's all right, Polly. I'm not being driven out of anywhere. I came here for the grass. Just for the grass.

"Moffitt, get on your horse and ride over for Denison. Bring Brown and that Kopke fellow, too. They say they buried him. We'll find out."

"Everything's getting cold," said the cook. "Come and get it! Damn it to hell, why do you have to start an argument at suppertime? You eating here or at Arbogast's?" he asked Broadbaker.

"Have the boy bring something to the wagon. No neck meat. Not much gravy. Are you coming, Polly?"

"I'm not hungry. Why would they say they buried him if they didn't?"

"If he tried to kill me, I'd have to hang him. They probably thought they were saving his life."

* * *

It was half an hour before Moffitt came back with a group from the emigrant wagons. Their leader, a lanky, redheaded man named Denison, looked frightened and he acted tough to hide it.

"He's dead all right," Moffit said. "They buried him. They all say so."

"Let them say it," said Broadbaker.

"He's dead and buried," said Denison. "Why? What's all the excitement?"

Glass said, "I talked to him in the hotel at Lodgepole day before yesterday."

There was a tight silence.

"I have some papers he signed. My partner saw him, too. This won't hold up, fellows. You hauled him there."

"Well, all right! We found out at the last minute that he was still breathing,

39

so we hauled him to town. We didn't want to say anything. We thought it would just stir up more trouble."

"You told me he was dead," shouted Broadbaker.

"I figured he'd die. We all figured it."

"But you told me he was dead. I want that, by God, to be made clear."

"I'm making it clear."

"All right. I want everybody here to understand I had no way of knowing he was alive." He looked all around. "How about it? Is there anybody in doubt?"

Denison went on. "And he claimed by the gods that he didn't try to ambush you or anybody. He said he wasn't anyplace near your wagon."

"Are you calling me a liar?" asked Grand in a pleasant-deadly tone. "Is that — "

"I'm not calling you anything. I'm telling what Kid Maybee said. As far as I can see, it's your word against his word."

"How about my word?" asked Ellis Moffitt.

"Never mind," said Broadbaker. "We can't settle it tonight. Glass!" He walked and faced him. "There's no reason I owe you an apology. It was a misunderstanding, pure and simple."

"That satisfies me. I'm taking over his herd. Eight hundred, more or less. And the horses and wagons. I want this all clear. And I'm heading north to Montana."

"Tonight?" said Broadbaker, laughing.

"No, I'm a bit weary tonight."

He watched without seeming to as Polly Argobast swept everyone with her angry gaze, turned, and walked off. He had never seen anyone walk so straight. She was a tight bundle rolled up in the riding skirt, and her spine was like a gun barrel. As she walked she flicked off grass heads with vicious little cuts of her quirt.

5

How to Get Rich in the Cattle Business

HE ate, drank strong coffee, and after lying for a while on the ground with his boots toward the fire, he found he was so tired from riding that he could scarcely move. Besides, his jaw ached, and he could tell by the tenderness and the heat that it was slightly swollen.

"Is it lopsided?" he asked a young cowboy named Seers.

"Not bad. He batted you one."

"He delivers a good blow."

"You took it pretty good, too."

"Better than Maybee?"

The cowboy didn't want to talk about it, and Glass couldn't blame him. He didn't have any nine thousand dollars at stake, only forty a month, grub pile, and a flat place to roll up in his blankets.

He moved around the camp and talked to others. It was a hard-bitten crew but friendly enough. Grand and his bunch, who called themselves scouts, although better described as Broadbaker's gunmen, kept to themselves, noisy and ribald, evidently with a supply of whiskey.

He located Maybee's supply wagons. There were two of them, or rather a wagon and a cart pulled tandem. His driver, the German kid, was a heavyset youth of about eighteen. His name was Otto Hoess. He told Glass he wanted to join an uncle who was a steam engine expert working in a town named Enterprise, somewhere near the border of Idaho. Glass did not know there were engines anywhere in the north territory except on the Missouri, and he had never heard of Enterprise, whereupon Otto showed him a letter, but it was written in German.

"Does Maybee owe you anything?"

"No, I work my passage."

He inventoried the supplies and had a look at the horses. The draft stock had been hobbled in some grass near camp, and Otto showed where he slept nearby.

"You're a good boy, Otto. If we get through to Montana, I'll see to it you have a few dollars."

"The boss wants to see you," said a cowboy.

"Where is he? In his wagon?"

"Yes."

He knew where he was. There was a candle burning, and his big shadow showed on the canvas every time he got up and walked around.

"Come in," said Broadbaker to his knock. He was seated at a table that let down from one wall on leather thongs. "Why are you going to Montana?" he asked.

"It wasn't me that decided it. It was Kid Maybee."

"Well, Kid Maybee isn't here. You're half owner and, what's more important,

44

you're in authority. How would you like a drink?" He got a bottle of whiskey and glasses. "If I could show you how you could be money ahead in the long run by sticking with me and the Arbogasts, oughtn't you do it?"

"Some of the cattle are his — ours — outright. But about half he gathered on shares with the understanding he'd sell them at gold camp prices, high as forty-two fifty. There's that promise involved."

"Glass, you're a fool. In the first place you'll never get your herd to Montana. You intend to start out across Cheyenne country with who for protection? Those waggoners! They're not fighters! They have women and kids along. They're underfoot, as far as I'm concerned. I let 'em come along because I felt sorry for them. They're doing me no favor. They aren't even decently armed. Their women are sick. Take 'em and go, but you have my sympathy. No army for your protection. The government has withdrawn from Fetterman and all the forts. According to the new treaty, the Sioux and Cheyenne have all the territory from the Black Hills to the Big Horn. They'll kill you all, make arrowheads out of your wagon tires, and this winter they'll be eating jerked beef instead of buffalo. I shouldn't give a damn. If you drive over the brink of hell, is it any skin off my nose?"

"I don't know."

He laughed, showing his powerful teeth. "You don't give me an inch or an ell, do you?"

"What do you want me to do?"

"I'd like to have you throw in with the Arbogasts and me and go to the Popo country. I scouted that range with my own eyes, and it's the best under the sun. Grass, by God, up to your belly. Water, and just a short drive south the Union Pacific. A few Indians on it, but if we don't take it, somebody else will. As for these emigrants, let them come if they'd like or go north if they'd like. Are you your brother's keeper? People like them are scattered all over the trail and they have to root hog or die."

"You make it sound pretty — tantalizing. You certainly do."

"Make it *sound*! I'm not trying to make it sound. I'm telling you how it is. Grass, water, protection from the winter. Deep snow, maybe, but, damn it, deep grass. The best elk country you ever saw. A rancher's paradise. I don't have to make it sound like anything. It *is*. And look at the market. Look how it's been going up and up since the Kansas City packing plants opened. I'm telling you how to get rich in the cattle business. But you think it over. Think it over before you're dead and the winter wind is howling through your ribs on Christmas day."

He did think about it. He thought about it for a long time as he lay on his back looking at the starry night. He was very tired. Too tired for sleep. His jaw ached throbbingly . . .

6

Across a Wide Land

THEY awoke before the sun. It was a gray dawn. The last star was just going out. The cook 'Frogs' Braskin, called for breakfast by beating a tin pan. Newcomers were always warned not to call him Frogs to his face. It referred to some joke played on him, several versions of which Glass was to hear in the days that followed.

Breakfast was taken on the go. Few sat down. Those who did ran danger of having dust kicked in their food. Men rode into camp, drank coffee scalding hot, and rode away holding pancakes rolled around pieces of grease-dripping bacon. The cookwagon was being packed while breakfast was being eaten, and it rolled away, careening over the hummocky flats to get a mile or two ahead of the rising, bawling, dirt-kicking cattle. Cowboys kept riding up and tossing their cups inside.

Otto was up, hitched and rolling. the Arbogast wagons were rolling. Everywhere wagons were taking their own routes across the land. One of the Arbogast boys was driving. He knew him by his manner of sitting, remembered him from long ago, riding in a buggy, women and champagne, colored boy hired to sit in back and play banjo. Polly Arbogast was riding fast as the wind to some destination. Her hair kept getting loose from her hat, and she kept tucking it back again.

Dad Haze came around and said, "Leo, do you know which brands are ours? I mean, the horses."

"Y2 on the left shoulder. It's the Kid's personal saddle string. It's down in the papers."

"I sure do need a fresh horse."

"Saddle one."

"And you?"

"I'll pick one out."

They were about the last to catch horses. The Y2 string ran to rangy grays and sorrels. None of them had been ridden for quite a while. They were well fed and willing to buck. He recognized the roan that the Kid had talked about and avoided him, although all the talk about a curb bit and being thrown into the side of a wagon was probably a lie. It was the story the Kid had concocted to account for leaving so as not to frighten Glass from taking the job.

"Good saddle string," said the wrangler. "They were galled when he came here, but I kept ointment on them, and they're in good shape now."

"They look like good long-horses."

"Yes, the Kid was one who liked to be able to travel night and day if somebody took out after him," he said for a joke.

It wasn't too much of a joke.

He counted the string and compared them with the inventory because the time would come when he'd have to give an accounting, and if one was astray or borrowed, he wanted to know it now.

"Where's the 'strawberry spotty rump'?"

"Lejune is riding him."

"Is he that half-breed with Grand?"

"Yes."

"What are you going to do?" asked Dad.

"I don't know. But they're not using horses from our string without asking."

"We're eating their grub."

"Not Billy Grand's grub. Anyhow, there's that stuff we brought on the packhorses. The cook's helping himself to whatever he needs."

"Just the same, we oughtn't go looking for more trouble."

"Who was it reached for his gun last night? That wasn't me, Dad. I just laid there on the ground."

"I didn't draw — I just wanted 'em to know you had some backing. Anyhow, I think we're foolish to go on staying here. I mean, in Broadbaker's camp. It sets us up for whenever he wants to bushwhack us. I think if we're in with those pilgrims, we ought to stay with those pilgrims."

The emigrant camp had finally broken up. All of their wagons were moving, though laggardly, with the last getting mixed among bawling cattle. Two kids were driving the remuda, which ran to heavy-legged draft stock. There was a belled cow. The bell sounded as if it had been made by putting a stone in an empty tin can.

"There's that cowbell again," the herd boss, a tough-faced trailer named Al Manning, said. "Those brainless hoe-men. They'll ring it some night and have this bunch to running. Is Broad around? He'll have to talk to Denison or somebody about that cowbell."

The cattle had a way of traveling in bunches. There was a main herd of about a thousand, which stayed together, and smaller bunches that kept wanting to strike out by themselves or balk for the grazing. These were the worst problem. A good third of the cowboys were needed to goad them on. It was dry on the creek bottoms. The dust rolled in white clouds and hung in the early sunlight. There were cutbanks on the west. The cattle were driven through gully slots in the banks, which became wider from their passage. The dirt of the prairie on top was harder, and the dust diminished, but by then it was hot. A wind came and blew strongly, shaking the grass and the sagebrush. The backs of the cattle were all white from dust. It formed cakes from their slobber. They would turn wall-eyed and bawl, and get their necks hung up over one another's backs and slobber. Then the drivers would come yelling *hi-ya*, goading them on again. At its greatest the herd strung out for about three miles, but they tried to keep them closer than that.

Led by Frogs Braskin, the wagons of the main camp headed straight out in front, with the lead steers following after about half a mile. The emigrant wagons tended more and more to the south and kept turning that wing of the herd. After a time, all moving well, Glass rode to the highest ground, a gentle swell that here and there became a ridge with a reef of sandrock showing. The view was all but endless. Far, far to the north was a blue line that looked like little, flat-topped buttes. That was the rise of land beyond the Platte and the Sweetwater. The old Oregon Trail. Between the ground sloped and broke into little rises and sloped again, and the shadows of clouds could be seen passing across it. The horizon was so vast it was inexhaustible. The horizon was not a line but a lace where the land and sky merged without definition. It was a place where there were clouds and mountains intermingled, and the longer you looked, the deeper you could see, and whole new areas sorted out — plains and hills and dry rivers and badlands, the white shine of alkali that might be dry lake bed, a dry pothole of one mile in extent, and the plumes of dust devils and smokes. There was always a prairie fire somewhere, and sometimes, at night particularly, you could smell the pines of the mountains.

7

Night Visit

THERE was no water, only a few seepage places quickly stirred to deep mud by the herd. The country became progressively parched as the slopes of the Laramies were left behind. In the evening Billy Grand and his scouts rode in with a packhorse and a small keg of spring water lashed to its back. It was delivered to Broadbaker's wagon. The others made out on the warm, flat stuff from the cookwagon tank, brown from oak tannin and with a gas-sulphurous taste.

The breed, Lejune, was riding a spotty rump horse, Y2 branded.

"Good horse, Lejune."

Lejune watched Glass without answering. Men stood and sprawled on the ground, watching to see what would happen. Lejune had a face like a hawk and very narrow-set eyes. He had an Indian's way of revealing nothing, nothing whatever.

"You didn't ask me before you rode that horse."

"My horse!"

"He's Y2 branded. How do you explain that?"

Billy Grand said, "Lejune bought him. He bought him from Maybee."

"Let's see the papers."

"He can't read and write. It was verbal."

"Then he can ride him verbal."

"You're not accusing me of making this up, are you?"

"Grand, Broadbaker knocked me flat on the ground to point up that same sort of idea last night, and I didn't do a thing. But that was because he was the boss. You're not the boss."

Taking his casual time, he turned his back on them. He walked off, and Dad Haze said, "That set it up. This is what they're waiting for. You'll get it in the back like Kid Maybee."

"I don't believe it. Not while Broad thinks I may go to the Popo."

He went to Broadbaker's wagon. Only the driver was there. Later Broadbaker came around and found him. "Were you looking for me?" he asked.

"Yes. Your breed, Lejune, claims he bought that spotty-rump Y2 horse from Maybee. Grand and some of your scouts are willing to say it was a verbal agreement. That's my horse unless they got papers saying otherwise."

"You're using a lot of my stuff. You're eating your grub at my wagon. I pay the cook. There has to be some sharing."

"Well, let him ask. I'm telling you, Broad, because I don't want you to come around complaining that I killed one of the men you'll need to shoot the Indians off that grass on Popo Agie."

★ ★ ★

The camp quieted. It was unusually quiet, but the cattle, unwatered, were restless. There was some lightning too distant for thunder. Dark clouds passed along the western horizon and faded without a trace. The night wind carried the odor of grass and sage unlocked by coolness.

Someone came up through the shadows. He had stopped beyond the cookwagon. There was a fire or the banked coals of a fire and a dull glow of heat on the coffee pot. Riders breaking their night circle often came in to pour a cup of coffee and sit on their heels for a while drinking it. Glass sat in bed, waiting. It was very quiet. Over the night sound of cattle he could hear the wolves. The man walked on. Not one of Grand's bunch. It was one of the men from the emigrant camp.

Glass got up. He slept in pants and sox and his hat half on his head and half wadded beneath because the nights were cold even in midsummer, so all he needed to do was pull on his boots. He got his gun and carried it with the belt swinging.

"Hello!" he said.

The man started suddenly and said, "Oh, you! I was looking for you."

"I been around all day. I saw you not a hundred feet away when we were crossing that last gully."

"The fellows want to talk."

"What fellows?"

"Over at camp."

"Did you walk?"

"Yes."

"I'm not much for walking. I took up this line of work because I could do everything on the back of a horse."

He meant it to be amusing, but the man was grim serious. He was a short, dehydrated man with the manner of one with alkali in his veins. His name was Alexander. They called him Alex. Glass didn't know whether Alexander was his first name or his last. They walked for several minutes. There was a fire that appeared to be burning in a peculiar manner, white-hot and dim, and sounds of clanging iron. The fire was being used as a forge, with a hand bellows brightening the sagebrush coals.

"We were in hopes you'd show up without us coming around," said Alex. "It would have looked better."

"What do you mean, looked better?"

"Like maybe you was on our side."

"I'm not on your side or anybody's side except *my* side."

"You're taking over for Maybee, aren't you?"

"Yes."

"Well, he was on our side. But look what it got him! Go ahead and say it. Look what it got him."

"I wasn't going to say it."

"Anyhow, we managed to save his life. We hauled him to that town — what was the name of it?"

"Lodgepole."

"Yes, Lodgepole. All these Wyoming towns are Indian-named. And the cricks named after drought and poison. Spider Crick, Poison Spider Crick, Rattlesnake

Crick, Dry Crick, Powder Crick, Alkali Crick, Bone Crick — "

"There's the Little Muddy — that's pretty wet."

Alex fell to cursing the country. He did it as from long practice, the words coming out of him by rote. It could have been taken down as sort of an outline of profanity.

"What happened to him?"

"Didn't Maybee tell you?"

"He didn't tell me much of anything."

"They quarreled. Him and Broadbaker. He was going to cut loose and drive for the Bozeman road, and Broadbaker refused to stop the herd. Broadbaker knocked him down. Then he almost kicked his head off. He was unconscious, and he just kept kicking him. You could actually see the blood signs from his boots right there on the grass. I don't know what happened next. I don't put any stock in Grand's story about ambush. It was an excuse to kill him. I don't know, and none of us do, but we all think Broadbaker ordered him shot. It stands to reason. If the Arbogasts weren't along, he'd probably have us all killed and be done with it. But he needs the influence of the Arbogasts. The old judge is still a big name in Washington. He needs the judge on his side when it comes to dealing those poor Injuns off their reserve at the Popo."

Then they came up to the emigrant camp with its wagons, two-wheeled carts that had been made from wagons, and horses grazing, picketed and hobbled, in the moonlight.

"By God, when I think I voted for Judge Arbogast!" said Alex. "Three times I voted for him."

"Where is he? — not in Wyoming."
"Oh, no! he's living in Omaha in style — on Broadbaker money. He just sent Lon and that girl. Can you imagine him turning that girl over to Broadbaker?"

8

The Wagon Smasher

HE recognized Denison. He walked on and was introduced to men by the names of Archer Beer, Chuck McCoy, and Kopke, Brown, Pattison, and Frye. Brown was a preacher. He didn't look like it. A farmer preacher, self-ordained. Frye was a small rancher from down in Kansas and owned about four hundred head of stock. The others owned fifty or a hundred or none at all. Most of them were farmers who had not made a go of it and were looking for new homes, but Beer was a mill sawyer, and Kopke a heavy-iron smith, both hoping for new opportunities in the gold and silver camps of the north.

He learned these facts in the casual conversation over coffee before the real subject was raised.

"How about it?" asked Denison suddenly. "Are you for us or against us?"

"I'm for me."

This brought an angry, guttural response from broad-handed, leather-aproned Kopke, fresh from the forge, but Denison held up his hand.

"Wait. I'm for me, too. We're all for us. Broadbaker is for himself, and the Arbogasts are for themselves — that's why they tossed in with Broadbaker. Let's not call the kettle black. How much did Kid Maybee tell you?"

Alex said, "He didn't tell him a damn thing."

"He said to head for Montana."

"All right, here it is. We all joined up with the Broadbaker-Arbogast herd temporarily. We figured we'd get protection against the Kiowas, Sioux, and whatever until we were within range of the old Oregon Trail forts. As soon as we got to the Bozeman trail, we'd turn off for the north. Three

Forks, the Yellowstone, the gold camps. We have, all told, thirty-three rifles to fight off the Cheyennes. Indians don't steal cattle, preferring buffalo. We figured we could get through in a month. Twenty days if we drove like hell."

"The Bozeman Trail!" Archer Beer said bitterly. "Well, that's past and gone."

"Right. That was what brought on the row. Broadbaker guided away south. He kept mountains between us and the Bozeman turnoff."

"Why didn't you cut out and go?"

He laughed. "You know the answer. The cows are mixed up and dust-covered, so the devil himself couldn't read their brands. It'd be a two-day job for all hands, his included. I tell you it's a hell of a lot easier to get a herd like this moving than it is to get 'em to stop. When they do stop, it's night. And if Broadbaker has his way, all hell can't stop 'em. We're going, by God, on to the Popo Agie. He's decided it.

He's set his mind to it."

On the whole they looked like such a beaten-out lot that he couldn't imagine Broadbaker caring one way or the other. He indicated as much, although not calling them a beaten-out lot.

"No, he wants us there, busted wagons and all. I'll tell you why. That's Shoshone land over there where he's headed. The best grass in Wyoming, and only a two, maybe three-day drive down to the railroad. But Shoshone land by treaty. To make it worse, the Shoshones are officially signed-and-sealed friends of the whites. How will it look when a man, one-time officer of the damn Rebs, comes in and spreads his cattle, doing it in the teeth of the Indian agents and the Army? So he has to have help. Backed by enough white people, loyal Northerners, and he can do it. That's why he made a good deal with the Arbogasts. Judge Arbogast, friends in Washington, good friend of President Grant, and I don't know what all.

The Arbogasts were liquored out and whored out, but they still have plenty of influence. Mortgages and political influence. Are you beginning to see how it was to work? Commencing to see how we could help him?"

"In fact, you're looking better all the time."

"You bet! We're white settlers, voters, people with friends back east. One white man's got more voice than fifty Indians. Why, Broad might even give us a few cows, might let us take hold and grow some turnips. It could be we could fence a cornfield and build a shack without being killed and burned inside it. We protect him, and he protects us. He might start a store and sell us stuff. He might start a townsite. He might get a road up there and a coach line. He might end up being king of west Wyoming, and us his faithful people. Sort of like kind old Mars' what's-his-name and Uncle Tom."

"Has he talked to you about all this?"

"Just to me and Frye because we got pretty good herds of cattle. He's leaving the others with no choice."

"The others — you men without cattle — can't you pull out and drive your wagons where you want to?"

"Look at the wagons! Walk around and look at the wagons. Wheel sprung, rawhide, every night stop and weld iron, make spokes of cottonwood — how long can such outfits keep going? How far would they roll toward the gold camps?"

"You mean he's taking you the rough way?" Kopke, the heavy-iron smith, had a slight German accent, and that and his strength added violent emphasis to his words, which he emphasized by driving his fist in his palm. "He is deliberate, day by day, day by day, smashing our wagons! Wearing out stock! Forcing us over rocks! Down worst coulees! Smash! Bang! Over the foothill rims, where everything is steep, inside of the prairie, where everything is easy. Instead of the road, where campfires you can see at night. Day by day, by day, he is making us into beggars, beggars, beggars!"

9

Girl in the Moonlight

KOPKE returned to his improvised forge, and Glass started back to his blankets. It was nearly midnight by the moon. When you had slept outside enough, you became able to tell by the moon's size, its brightness, and the clouds what time it was. In the very middle of night the clouds were translucent, and looking at the moon through them was like viewing it through smoky quartz. But the first glow of morning made the clouds like clots of smoke. Still later the clouds would fade. They would become a vapor of nothing, and then the ground would grow dark, and the horizon light. When you were used to it, you never needed a watch. At least not in the summer, when the nights were short. In Wyoming, the high country, they were the shortest of anyplace he had ever been. In Montana he had heard they were even shorter. Along the Canada border the June nights were supposed to be only four hours long. By autumn the nights grew long, and you could no longer tell time by the moon through clouds, but you could often guess by the wind, warm at first and chilling, and the smell of things.

You couldn't have told by the smell tonight, he thought, because all he could smell were cattle. The swing herd — it was called that because it always drifted to the up country and had to be brought around in the evening — was bedded down on the south side, and hence the pilgrim camp was nearly surrounded.

Pattison's wife was sick. He had heard the men talking about it. She had a bed in the wagon and lay all day while it pounded across the prairie. If you rode close, you could hear her moaning. Even when the wagon was stopped, she continued her moaning.

"How's your missus?" he had asked Pattison. "I hear she's sick."

"Oh, tolerable." But he knew by the man's beaten-out, weary tone that she was not tolerable at all. "She's sick with what her sister had. The gallstones. It helps when she can lie out straight and drink willow tea. But this God-awful prairie isn't helping her at all. Sometimes we get to the flat gumbo, where it's soft. Like old lake beds. That's fine. But this bunch grass is like a washboard, only worse. One wheel at a time. It pains her fierce to be jounced around."

"If I were you, I'd say to hell with all this and drive her back to Cheyenne. They got a doctor, a Chinaman, who's supposed to be good on gallstones. I heard some folks talking about it. He treats them with green herbs and gallons and gallons of soapy water and pretty soon he has a person all relaxed, every muscle as limp as a baby. And the gallstones just ooze out. I saw a fellow that carried his around in a buckskin bag. There were thirty-seven of them, from the size of peas on up to the marbles you use playing Kelly pool."

"Oh, God, but how would I get her to Cheyenne? It's two weeks back to Cheyenne."

"By trail drive but not by wagon. You could cut straight south and catch the U.P. passenger train at Fort Steele. You could take the trail right up the North Fork of the Platte."

"No, my wagon would never hold out." He didn't want to go by himself. As bad as this was, being cut off was worse. It was a peculiar thing, Glass noticed, but most people would endure anything rather than being cut off, and strictly on their own.

There was a candle burning in the sick woman's wagon. It made a dull pumpkin-colored glow through the canvas. Someone was with her. The candle went out, and the canvas looked gray-white under the moon. A girl got down from the wagon and was riding his way. He knew by the swing of her body that it was the Arbogast girl, the girl with the whip, Polly. He stood perfectly quiet, and she rode almost to him.

"Hello!" he said.

She reined in suddenly, and her hand dropped to the pommel of her saddle. A pistol was strapped there. "It's you," she said.

"Yes, ma'am."

"So you were at the meeting!"

"Yes."

"You're starting right where Kid Maybee left off, aren't you?"

"I'm doing nothing disgraceful. What's eating on you? I had nothing against Broadbaker or anybody when I came here. I enlisted to do a job on shares and I'm doing my best to make good on my agreement."

"I suppose you think it's a good idea to turn these wagons north for Montana, that poor woman as sick as she is!"

"I'm not making that choice. She sure wouldn't be any asset to me."

She was going to ride past, so he took hold of her bridle.

"Let go of that!"

"No, let me talk to you."

"Let go!"

"You going to hit me with the quirt? Or use the pistol? You'll have to do one. Otherwise I'm going to talk to you."

She looked down on him. Her lips were a tight line, and her small chin jutted.

"Why did it make you so almighty mad when I called Broadbaker on that killing back in Nebraska?"

"It was a damned, dirty lie, that was why! He never — "

"It was damned and dirty, but it wasn't a lie. In fact, I don't think Broadbaker would deny it if you came out and asked him. You know what I think? I think you're ashamed of teaming up with him. You're ashamed that the mighty Arbogasts would have to accept his help. He's killing that gallstone woman."

"Let me go." She swung at him with the bridle reins, and he moved, making them miss.

"No, you listen to me. He's killing Mrs. Pattison because he wants to smash these wagons and get the whole crowd beaten down so that turning off to Montana or going anywhere except the Popo is out of the question. He's forcing them down to the point where they got to come to him for help and then, by God, he'll have them in the palm of his hand."

"For what? To take over their junk wagons and spavined stock?"

"No, he's got stock and wagons. He needs people. He needs people to occupy that country and build him an empire."

"An empire! You know what you are, you're a damned fool."

"Maybe, but that's not what I'm talkin' about."

"Smashing wagons!" She laughed.

"You believe it, too. That's why you were over there trying to doctor that woman. You feel the Arbogasts are partly to blame — "

"Get away from me!"

She lashed her horse, and the animal reared away and was off at a gallop.

Broadbaker was up, standing in the back door of his wagon, when Glass walked into camp. He made no movement. He was a dark shadow against the door, almost invisible. Polly Arbogast came up from another direction, having left her horse with the night remuda. She disappeared beyond one of the wagons, a door whispered shut, and all was silent. For a long while, as long as Glass watched, Broadbaker stood in the door.

Glass slept, but he was troubled and dreaming. He sat up, thinking about what Alex had said. There was no truth to his remark that Polly Arbogast had been 'turned over' to anybody. She was certainly not Broadbaker's woman. But it was none of his business, anyway. She hated him like poison, and he had no interest in her. The only interest he took in Polly Arbogast as a woman stemmed from his dislike of Broadbaker. But it was galling to imagine her going to his wagon. It made him sweat and feel sleepless and thirsty.

He rolled over so as not to watch the wagon and thought, am I a fool? Why go to Montana? Just to oppose Broadbaker? Why not the Popo? With eight hundred head I'd be big enough to take care of myself. But, then, there were those pilgrims depending on him.

10

'Grit Your Teeth, Maw!'

THAT morning the cattle were up early. They were thirsty, pawing dust and bawling. Front runners were already on the move. The swing herd was angling toward the south and needed turning.

"Git your dough gods!" Frog Braskin was shouting. "Get it before I toss it to the wolves. We got to roll. If them cows get to water first, we'll have mud stew for supper."

"I just been checking up on the horses," said Dad.

"Did that breed take — "

"No, he took a little red bronc branded Hanging S. Where'd you go last night?"

"Over to the pilgrim wagons. How did you know I was gone?"

"I sleep with one eye open, that's how."

"You were snoring when I left."

"That may be, but I woke up afterward. I got a sixth sense for people walking up through the dark."

"I'll have to be quieter."

"Not you."

"Who, then?"

"Broadbaker. The Man-Eater. I woke up, and there he stood, looking at your bed. I thought he'd come around to kill you. But your bed was empty. I just laid there. I didn't make a move. It gave me the creeps. You know, I'm not scared of any man alive, but if I was going to be scared, I'd be scared of *him*."

Glass needed some clean sox and had to ride after the plunder wagon, which Otto was driving bounce and gallop over the prairie to get out in front of the dust. After changing sox, he rode in the wagon for a while, enjoying the warm, early sunrise. Everything was fresh, and the air was like cider. They topped a rise, and he could look back on all the herd, its main body and the side currents, spread below and away across a downward sweep of the country. The emigrant wagons had started late and were falling steadily behind. They looked gray through the dust.

It bothered him that he should ride in such comfort in the crystal of morning while the woman bounced in pain in the dust-choking wagon box, so he rode over. Pattison's thirteen-year-old kid was driving. He was gangling and freckled and underfed. He was dressed in cast-offs of his father's. The top had come free of his hat like the lid of a can and was held by one strip of felt and some crosshatch sewing. His hair was tangled and hung in burlap-colored locks down the back of his neck, but somebody had shear-hacked it off at the sides. He had a pair of boots made to fit a two-hundred-pound man. Not owning sox, he had wadded grass in the boots to take up the slack, and it stuck out in bits and shreds where the toes were gone and a side ruptured.

The wagon, in general, looked as bad as he did. The tongue was split and bound with rawhide; the wheels were sprung where the spokes had been replaced with cottonwood, and the cottonwood had dried and warped. Riding up behind the wagon you could see all the wheels wobbling, each with its own rhythm. It would have been funny under other circumstances. Even the other emigrant wagons seemed to avoid the Pattisons. He could hear the woman moaning. She did not moan loudly but steadily and drearily, as if each dip of the worst wheel, the off-side hind one, had pushed it out of her.

Pattison was inside the wagon. He came and stood at the back, bracing himself against the rock and looking out at him.

"How is she?" Glass asked.

"Same."

"Have you got any medicine?"

"We gave her pain killer and we gave her laudanum, but none of it seems to do much good. The laudanum is some good, but it binds her fearsome."

"Did Polly bring anything?"

"Who?"

"Polly Arbogast."

"Yes, she brought some medicine. It was her brought the pain killer. I was wondering if maybe there'd be another China doctor up in Casper — if we got that way."

"There'd be an army surgeon at the fort."

"But he'd want to operate. I'm not for that. It's against our religion. It is the will of Jehovah not to shed blood."

He could hear the woman inside asking her husband who it was he was talking to?

"The fellow that Maybee sent. Now lie down, Maw."

"No, I want to see him. Zeke, I want to talk to him."

"Lie down, Maw. You know you can't stand."

"Stop, then. Tell him to come to the door."

Glass could see her inside the wagon, lying on a thick grass mattress and crazy quilts. The sun came in beams through the side rents of the canvas and shone on the dust that rose through the floor. She was wild-haired and haggard, and with crazy eyes. She was probably no more than thirty-five, although she looked sixty.

"Pull up!" she was saying. "Tell Will to pull up."

The boy stopped, and she said to Glass, "Who is this doctor that treats you with herbs? How can I get to him?"

"He's a Chinese doctor back in Cheyenne."

"Oh, I'd never go to a heathen. Oh, dear God, can't we rest for a while? I wish we could get where it wasn't so bumpy. Oh, for some blessed trees and shade! If we only had some cold water. Oh, God, why did we ever leave home?"

"Keep rolling," Pattison said to his boy. "You got to make out, Maw.

85

You just got to grit your teeth and make out."

"Ain't there some smoother road?"

"No, there ain't any smoother road, Maw."

The wagon banged onward; and again, steadily, she moaned.

11

Hell's Crossing

LEO GLASS was young, he had a good horse under him, and there was the endless sweep of God's own country beckoning him. Under those circumstances it is not always easy to concern oneself with people like the Pattisons. It was a severe temptation to simply ride and get the wind in your face and forget that they ever existed. Why did they start out in a broken outfit in the first place? It was their damn fault. Pattison was lazy as dirt. He's made a career of being a millstone about other peoples' necks. This is a tough country. It's root hog or die. You can't sacrifice everybody for the sake of one weakling. You have to be tough in order to be kind. All these things came into his mind, and it took an effort to push them out again.

They were crossing a high prairie that sloped gently to the north. The drop was nowhere more than eighty feet to the mile, but a remarkable foreshortening took place because of the clarity of the air, and at eighteen or twenty or thirty miles the declivity seemed very great, an ocean drained of water in which buttes floated like flat-topped islands. Here and there the prairie was cut by a dry watercourse. These were customarily steep-sided, but the wagons could cross on the old buffalo routes. The buffalo trails were often as good as roads, just wide enough for a wagon, winding but quite smooth, and handy places to pick up buffalo chips for the evening's fuel. But here and there a coulee had cut itself a chasm that did real justice to the size of the country. Commencing far out on the flatland, it would work its way back by headward erosion, not all at once but by cycles, with the final rims a quarter to a half mile apart, enclosing pinnacles, cutbanks, gullies, eagle's nests, timber, coyotes, small game, grizzly bears, and rattlesnakes, with perhaps a tiny stream, its pothole residues, or even a spring or two in the bottom. Some of the courses started out as creeks in the mountains, and if so, they were called creeks, water or not, but most of them commenced suddenly with a cirquelike hole in the prairie at the confluence of several minor gullies and as such were not dignified by being called this-or-that coulee. They were true canyons, however, and aside from rivers in flood and mountains the major obstruction to travel.

A great coulee — the Malpheer — brought the cookwagon to a halt early in the afternoon. There was a road of sorts or what looked like a road, although closer inspection showed it to be the twin travois marks of an Indian crossing. The ruts were characteristically wider than a wagon gauge, although the squaws could narrow them when need be. In some places the travois grooves had served as channels for the runoff, so it was not unusual to see one of them several feet deep, while the other looked like a perilous footpath, or both might end at a sudden cutbank, and a stranger to the land might ponder why a road had ever been put there — or how.

"Is this the Malpheer?" Old Dad asked, riding up beside Glass, who had reached the spot. "How does it look?"

"Deep."

"Deep and steep," he agreed.

There were wagons all along the rims and men out testing the ground.

"This is going to be hell to cross," said Dad. "I've had experience in such things. You got to get out and try every foot of it by tromping, or otherwise what looks like a solid way will just crumble and go to hell. You can lose horses, wagons, everything. Don't we have a guide? I thought there was some squawman named Gaines. Have you ever met him?"

"He comes in at night, from what I hear. I imagine he leaves his information with Broad and then rides out again. They're pretty much lone-wolfers, those guiders."

The first cattle were bawling close, and several riders came up with their handkerchiefs still tied over their noses. One and all they were covered from head to toe with silvery gray dust.

One of them asked, "Why do we cross up here? Why don't we cross the low country, where it's easy? Yonder this widens out and is nothing on the flatland. You can see it from here."

"I ain't worried. My bronc will get me down. He's surefooted as a mule. And if he can't carry me, I'll get off and carry him."

"How'd you like to get that old wagon of what's-his-name — the fellow with the sick wife? — how'd you like to drive that rig down?"

"Sidewise or endwise?"

"With the wheels on it I'd rather try it sidewise."

"They say she's got the gallstones. This is likely to jar 'em right out of her."

Most of the riders were a mere nineteen or twenty years old, looking for adventure in the great northwest, and Glass, who was twenty-seven, was able to smile tolerantly at their cruel jokes.

They commenced laying bets as to whether the Pattison wagon would get to the other side and then whether Broadbaker would try crossing at all.

"He'll go across," said Dad. "He's bullheaded enough to drive this spread right over the rim of hell."

The cookwagon was already down the first pitch and it had stopped there while Braskin was testing the next segment of crooked travois trail.

"Hey, Frogs, why don't you narrow that wagon down a bit?" the fellows were yelling at him but not loud enough so he'd be likely to hear.

There was a man on horseback about a hundred yards below. Short and heavy, with a great faceful of black whiskers and his hair a tangle down his back, garbed in moccasins and fringed buckskin left open because of the heat, he was gesturing, showing Braskin the route down. This was Gaines, the guide.

"It's all right," he called, cupping hands. "We'll snub the wheels at the last drop, but the rest you can take with the hand brake."

"Here goes three hundred dollars worth of wagon," called a teamster in charge of a load of supplies, and with some urging got his team to follow the cookwagon. The cookwagon moved on, and one outfit after another followed.

There was no danger as long as the brakes held out. But if they didn't the horses would have to run or be run over, and it would end with a smashed wagon, scattered supplies, and worst of all, broken-legged horses that had to be destroyed.

"All right, let's get these wagons down before the cattle get here," Broadbaker said, riding up on a big-barreled bay. He began signaling, making wide sweeps with his hat. "Hey-ya! Come on! Don't let a dry wash like this stop you. You're not in Nebraska now. These are the Rocky Mountains. This is nothing to what we'll have to cross later on. Come on and roll! Roll! There'll be worse than this on the way to the Popo. Set your brakes at the edge and get the horses moving! The secret is to go! Go! Go!"

Dad said, "You going to let that German kid take the wagon over?"

"He's our driver. Go ahead, Otto!"

Without hesitation Otto drove to the edge and over. One after another the wagons hit the first sag skidding and came to a stop amid clouds of dirt. There was a turning and almost level going for a few yards and then another slope. Winding and balancing the trail then took them along a minor ridge, and this, by a sudden drop-off to the next bench.

Some of the emigrant group had driven along the edge farther up, and there seemed to be an argument.

Broadbaker rode over and yelled, "Keep going!" He saw Glass and said, "These are your people. Keep 'em moving."

When Glass tried to tell him that most of their wagons were in no shape to take such a crossing, Broadbaker wouldn't listen.

"What the hell? They claim I'm trying to destroy their outfits. Then when I try to get across before the cattle, they stall and do nothing. If you want to go down by a road, go! If you'd prefer to go after four thousand cattle tramp out what road there is, do that! But don't come around and yell Man-Eater to me!"

Denison drove up with his wagon and cart hitched tandem and started the descent. His outfit was good enough, but the car had no brakes or man to snub the wheels. Loaded, it outraced the wagon, pulling the whole outfit around and almost rolling over.

"Are you bossing this bunch or is anybody?" Broadbaker shouted, his countenance distorted with fury.

"Dad, come here and send these outfits over, will you?"

He rode back to the Pattison's. The kid was still driving. HIs father was at some distance, riding an old mare bareback, trying to get the family's crowbait stock together.

"Do you think you can manage this?"

"I'll drive!" said the kid, scared sick.

Glass rode out and said, "Pattison, how about your wife? You can't take her down there."

"Well, what am I going to do?"

Glass had no answer.

"She can't ride and she can't walk."

"Goddammit — "

"If you got any better idea for getting Pauline down there, let's hear it."

"How are your brakes?"

"They're brakes! I put new rawhide shoes on them. They hold better than hickory."

Pattison's would be about the last wagon over. The big, brindle lead steer that always pointed the herd was only a couple of hundred yards away. Then he saw the wagon belonging to Jack Brown.

"Brown!" he called through cupped hands.

Brown stopped, and they tried to exchange shouts, their voices lost in bawling, distance, and confusion. In the meantime Mrs. Pattison had pulled herself to the rear of the wagon and looked out.

"I ain't going to move. I ain't going to leave this wagon. I'd rather just die here."

Polly Arbogast, riding over at a gallop, called to Glass, "She can't ride down in that."

"You try to talk to her."

"That old wagon — it'll fall to pieces — "

97

"Well, tell that to Broadbaker," cried Pattison. "He's the one that brought us here. He chose this place instead of the easy going to the north. He intended to kill us. Well, Thy will be done."

"Where's *your* wagon?" Polly asked Glass.

"It's halfway to the bottom by now."

"No, I'm not going to leave," wailed Mrs. Pattison. "Zeke, don't let 'em take me away."

"It's all right, Maw, I'll get you to the bottom."

"It's downhill all the way," muttered Dad.

Glass shouted, "I'll follow you. When we get to the first bench, I'll see about finding some help . . . "

But with the cattle pressing close, Pattison took over the driver's seat, letting the kid ride the mare, tested the brakes, and drove over.

The wagon made it well on the first pitch. Pattison, with his boots set, placed his weight on the hand brake. The hind wheels skidded all the way. His first trouble came when he released the brake to roll for a few yards and then applied it again. This time one of the shoes held tight, but the rawhide mending of the other gave way. With one wheel turning and the other locked, the wagon overran the rump of the off-wheeler, and the poor beast, after falling to his haunches, tried to run. The wagon went twisting and careening, still with one wheel locked and one free, and miraculously kept its balance by turning and sliding away from a dirt bank. And somehow it reached the second bench.

"Pull up!" Glass shouted. He called until he was hoarse with dust raw in his throat.

Pattison did not hear him. Amid his wife's screams and his own cursing he could hear nothing. He probably did not even realize he had reached the bench. Or maybe the horses could not have been stopped anyway. They kept going, and the second brake tore free. For a wild few seconds the wagon stayed in the tracks of its predecessors. The deep-pounded dirt of a little cut slowed it. Below, Kopke and Brown saw what was happening and came running both with a pole to ram through the rear spokes, but neither was in time. The team, old and weary though they were, had now been frightened beyond managing. The off-center wheel flopped back and forth with loose spokes banging the underframe. Then it collapsed, and the wagon dipped, digging a front axle into the ground. It plowed downward, turned completely around while the horses kicked their way free amid tangled and broken harness, a snapped tongue, and lashing whippletrees. And finally, very slowly, gently, the wagon tipped over on its side.

Pattison got to his feet. The broken reins were still in his hands. He had fallen on the downhill side of the wagon, and it had made a complete swing around him. He walked, long-limber legged, not seeming to know where he was. There was a gully with a two-foot dropoff, and he walked straight into it. Men helped him up and others carried his wife out of the wagon. They brought her out mattress and all. She was on her back, clinging to both sides and sobbing crazily.

"Get her out of here!" said Broadbaker. "Catch that team. I'll not have them charging into the herd and starting a run. Brown, Kopke, one of you fellows. Get her in your wagon and roll for the far side. When nobody moved to obey, he roared, "You sons of bitches! Do what I say. I'll kill you if you don't get a jump on. Get her loaded and out of here, or I'll let the herd tromp you six feet underground, where you belong."

12

Plan for a Showdown

ALTHOUGH Leo Glass was horseback and his mount was well shod and surefooted, the wagon had far out-raced him. He came up in the midst of Broadbaker's tirade and rode between him and the wreckage.

"We'll have to split the herd."

"I'll say if we split the herd," said Broadbaker.

"Say it, then, because it's what we're doing."

"Do you want her tromped to death?"

There was little danger of a stampede. Cattle spook on still nights when they are weary, thirsty, and perhaps nervous from some disquiet in the atmosphere. The hardest time to get anything like concerted action from cattle is when each is on its own, slip-sliding down banks, through brushy draws, specifically in a coulee cross such as this. So actually there was little danger that they would run and trample those caught in the midst of them. The thing to do was get some sort of obstruction up and move the woman behind it. They could hold a sheet or a blanket up to keep the heaviest dust off. A wet handkerchief over her face would help.

Lon Arbogast had stopped his wagon in the bottom. He put someone else in charge and got down. Broadbaker saw him and decided not to carry the dispute any further. Anyway, there was nothing he could do. Some of the cattle were coming down and being forked by the wreckage.

"Need some help up there?" asked Lon.

Broadbaker signaled him to go back, get the wagon, keep moving. He said to Glass, "All right, the responsibility is yours. If you want to keep her here, do it and be damned. This whole raggedy crew can be your responsibility."

"That son of a bitch," said Dad, looking at him ride away, stiff-legged and stiff-backed. "How I'd like to get my rifle out and take him off his horse."

"Never mind that. We better get some of the spilt stuff together before the cattle tromp it."

Provisions that had been roped in the wagon had come loose and scattered down the bank. A flour sack had burst. Several cans had broken loose and rolled all the way to the bottom. A trunk had ruptured, and bedraggled scraps of cloth, bonnets, old shoes, and a muff lay strewn.

"That's all my good fancywork!" she cried, sitting up. "Look, you're tromping on my fancywork. Oh, good God, can't I have anything nice? Can't I have a thing?"

"They're gathering everything up, Maw," said her husband. "Don't you worry. Things are going to be all right yet. You wait and see."

Somehow the herd passed, and the dust cleared away, and they got Mrs. Pattison to the far side of the now-roadless coulee in Kopke's wagon. It was afternoon then. They followed the beaten prairie left by the herd and came around by the south, where camp had been made. During the final hour Mrs. Pattison slept.

It was a weary and beaten-out camp. There was no water, only that left in the barrels, most of which had spilled from the hatch tops in the crossing of the Malpheer. There was no water to wash in, only dampened rags to get dust from your hands and face. The rags turned muddy black. You waited your turn at one of the wet rags and looked for a clean place to get the grit off your teeth. If you chewed tobacco, it got full of minute sand, and you had the sensation of sharpening your teeth.

"I feel like an old wolf," said a

bachelor named Ted Goings. "I been sharpening my fangs all day."

They envied Goings. He was alone and he had a good outfit. No kids to worry about. No women. He could cut out by himself anytime he liked — provided he was willing to abandon the twenty-seven head of stock, mostly bay Longhorn cows, which were mixed in with the main herd.

After supper, tired as they were, there was nothing to do except get to work once again on the wagons. Every outfit was overloaded. Things had been thrown away to lighten, but they were still overloaded and in need of repair.

"If we could just get up to the Platte," Denison said. "If we could lay to for a day and run these outfits into the mud for twenty-four hours. This dry weather has shrunk them so every joint is loose. A good swelling in water would tighten 'em up like axe handles and prevent three-fourths of the breakage. There's hardly been a sprung spoke or a thrown tire that couldn't have been prevented by a good soaking."

"How about that outfit of Zeke's?" somebody said. "If you tried soaking all that cottonwood in his wheels, they'd turn to figure eights."

"By the way, where is Zeke?"

"His missis is with the Kopkes, temporary."

"Him and his boy went back with the team to see if they could save maybe the hind wheels and make a cart."

"We'd be ahead, all of us, if we just burned that wagon. We would have been ever since Nebraska."

Denison began beating on an iron kettle, hung bell-like, the familiar gathering call.

Archer Beer, hearing it, stood up at his wagon and said, "Are we going to have another meeting? Talk, talk, talk! What is left to talk about?"

"You go on over there, Arch," said his wife, "and this time give 'em a piece of your mind. You tell 'em it's time to quit talking and do something. You tell 'em it's time to get all together, shoulder to shoulder, with guns in your hands, and march over and demand an accounting. You tell 'em it's time to stop this herd and cut our cattle out and head north for the road."

"Oh, you don't know what you're talking about. It's no use. Not tonight. We're in a dry camp. We can't stop and cut the herd here."

"Well, where *can* you?"

"I don't know!" he shouted. "That goddamn woman," he said when he came up to Denison's wagon, "she always knows what I ought to do. Well, I don't know what to do. Maybe I ought to give in and go to the Popo. Maybe Broadbaker or the Arbogasts would lend me enough to get started."

"They'd lend you nothing," said Denison. "You could work for 'em the rest of your natural life just like back home. It was what we were trying to get away from, remember? The railroad, the bank, and people like Andy Broadbaker. Only this time we'd be worse off. Because there'd be nobody, absolutely, that we could turn to. No, sir! I'm going north where a willing man can earn *ten dollars a day* in the gold mines. Do you know what ten dollars a day is? It's as much in one season as you could make in eight years shoveling another man's spuds and herding his cows."

"Yah, I know," he said wearily. "And don't tell me they ain't getting it, because I talked to men that knew. And it's right here in the St. Louis paper. *Captain Markey's Report on the Yellowstone Gold Mines.* There was one case where the operators from one gulch actually kidnapped the workers in another, paying them big wages. And not only that, a man with a team of horses can cash in. It's possible for a man with a helper and a team of horses to make *thirty dollars a day*. Why, money means nothing up there. They dig it out of the ground. Most people go up there and just toss it to the wind. But you don't have to.

There's nothing to stop you having a little garden, putting your missus and kids to work tending it, milking a cow, and saving every cent. A couple or three years of that and you could be on easy street. You could come back home and invest in a good little place and have it free and clear."

"I know, I know, but we're like rats caught in a trap. All that cheese is outside the wire."

"We're going to smash through that wire!"

Beer tried to rise with enthusiasm. He really tried. He knew it was as rough for Denison as it was for him, that he had traveled as far and got as thirsty and was as sweat-stuck and dirty and tired. He knew that if he was as good a man as Denison, he would jump up and say, 'Goddamm it, yes!' But he just couldn't do it. He just wasn't that good a man.

"Oh, son of a bitch," he said. "I'm just so beaten-out, alkied-out, sweated-out tired."

"You'll be all right tomorrow. There's thunder again. Maybe we'll get some rain."

It was hard to hold a meeting when most of the men were as discouraged as Beer. Then there were the natural jealousies — of Kopke, who had the best wagon, — being the only competent blacksmith, he repaired his own metal first; of Frye, who owned 400 head of stock and was naturally tempted to string along with Broadbaker; of McCoy, who had 150; of Goings, who had no family to tie him down, a good wagon, and some said $250 in cash hidden in it. And there was resentment that nobody had offered to make room for Pattison and his ailing wife, so that each thought the other was looking at him, thinking *he* ought to do it.

" . . . the point is, we can't go on without some kind of a *plan*," Denison was saying. Maude Beer says we got to go over there shoulder to shoulder with guns in our hands and she's right. But

111

we got to decide *when* to do it and *how* to do it. And then we got to *do* it. But it has to be done *right*. Like an attack in the army. Yes, just an act of war."

"Are *you* going to shove a gun in his guts, Denison?" asked a beat-out emigrant named Loughman, not hiding a bitter derision.

"I'll do it if I have to. Are you saying I haven't the nerve to do it?"

"*I'll* do it!" said Kopke.

"How about that fellow Glass? He's supposed to be a real ring-tailed terror when he gets started. Why don't *he* do something?"

"Maybe he will."

"And maybe he won't. There's plenty of *maybe* about him. Like his partner. Kid Maybee, catch on? Glass saw what happened to Kid Maybee and wants none of the same. Broadbaker knocked him flat on his behind the first night. And what did he do? Not a thing. Not a blessed thing."

"Furthermore, that girl is working at him," said Beer. "Whenever he rides out someplace, you keep watch, and there she is. I wouldn't be surprised if they were sneaking out in a coulee together. I know for a fact they met after dark that first night. I saw 'em right out on the prairie."

"Keep quiet, Beer. You carry that kind of talk around and you'll get killed. Arbogast, Broadbaker, or Glass — none of 'em is going to stand for it."

"Well, I didn't intend it should go any further."

Frye stood up and said, "What's this coming?"

It was a team and a white-topped wagon. There were mutterings of surprise. It was Glass and his supply wagon.

"Where's Pattison?" he asked.

They told him.

"He'll have to use this. His woman can have her bed in it right now. I made a deal for a cart belonging to the Arbogasts, and there are the packhorses. I wish Pattison was here."

"He'll be here directly."

With a load of junk, they were all thinking. Why was the poorest skate outfit the greatest collector of junk? He carried more weight then Goings or even Kopke, and it was mostly throw-away junk.

"We were just having a meeting," said Denison. "We've decided we have to face those people."

"You mean face up to Broadbaker."

"Right! We got to collide with Broadbaker. It's come to the point of kill or be killed."

"Not quite," Glass replied. "It has to be done at the right place and the right time. We can't do it at a dry camp and we can't do it tomorrow or the day after that. We got coulees and badlands to the north of us, and the only clear route's to the west. We'll break off only when we have a clear trail north. That means it will have to be at the crossing of the North Fork. He'll be one day — one whole day — and half the night, too, pulling critters from the quicksand there and probably rope-hauling the wagons. We'll cut the herd there. We'll do it when they come up from the river, then drive north. The river will lead us straight in to Casper. We'll have a guide waiting for us."

"How can we have a guide waiting?" asked Beer.

"I'm heading up there, taking Mrs. Pattison. I'm asking that every man contribute ten dollars. That will give her some better than a hundred dollars for doctoring. The post surgeon may not charge her. If so, the Pattisons will have a little something to live on. So you can load her into the wagon. I'm starting tonight."

13

The Roadless Way to Casper

BROADBAKER had shrugged his shoulders when Glass told him he was emptying his wagon and driving Mrs. Pattison up to Casper.

"It's your wagon. If you load any supplies with mine, don't ever come looking for them again. You're welcome to eat on me, you've furnished your share, but when you pull out for Montana, it's like an orphan at her wedding. You just take your naked body."

"I got a cart from Lonnie."

He looked perhaps more lean-jawed than before, but all he said was, "If the Arbogasts can afford charity, that's up to them."

After Broadbaker went back inside his wagon and closed the door, Polly

Arbogast walked over. He guessed that she had been watching.

"You're not leaving alone with her, are you? I mean — she's so awfully sick."

He waited, thinking for a moment she would offer to go along. It was an unsteadying thought — her riding through the night in the seat beside him, the rub of her hip against his, the smell of her, of her windblown hair.

"Don't you want an escort? This is still Indian country. We could spare some of the men."

"No. I'll whop out of here tonight. I got a fresh team. This ridge seems to lead straight to the lower Malpheer. A good moon and we should make it there by dawn. We'll have a couple miles of badlands. No Indians there. They think the devil lives in the badlands and maybe they're right. Anyhow, the Cheyennes must be northeast on the buffalo hunt. I'll just drive straight on and with any luck reach Casper tomorrow night."

"What if she has another bad attack?"

"I'll take her folks, naturally. The boy, anyhow. I'd rather have him than old Zeke. He's a good boy."

"And you'll just leave her there?"

"Yes, and come straight back. I'll take a collection to pay for her keep. You can be the first to contribute."

She gave him $20, ten for herself and ten for her brother. With like amounts from himself and Dad she would have $40, and he ought to be able to collect $100 from the pilgrims. They all had a little cached away.

"Aren't you going to ask Broad?"

"For money? No, ma'am. I figure I'm pressing my luck as it is."

"He's a good man. He's not so cruel as you think."

"That's the best news I've heard."

"Good-bye," she said, and smiled at him as he climbed to the wagon seat. "You're a good man, too," she said.

"Thanks." And he drove away with

the sound of her voice as sweet as night music in his ear.

Zeke Pattison and his boy came back pulling the rear wheels and axle on which were roped and balanced two gunnysacks of wagon iron, the seat, endgate, some canvas, and two whippletrees.

"Give me a day or two, and I'd make a good cart," he said. "This was a real good wagon. It had forged iron in it, not cast. If we could stop here for a day or two and somebody would haul my old lady, I'd have me a cart that'd tote pound for pound with a wagon. I'd put a team of bulls and a cart up against a wagon and horses any day."

"Where's Maw?" the boy asked.

"Glass is taking her to Fort Casper," said Denison.

"Who says he is? This is pretty high-handed."

"You haven't any choice, Zeke. She can't take this kind of a beating any longer. The only question is, are you going with her?"

"I can't leave all this stuff. This is all the property I got in the world. How about my stock?"

"We'll care for it."

When he heard that a fund of more than $100 had been raised, he quickly gave in and made ready to go. Glass would rather have had just the boy, but he couldn't object, and it was best for Mrs. Pattison to have her husband along.

"Don't you want me to help drive?" he asked Glass.

"No, you stay with your missus. Willard will help me."

"I'll expect you to make it right with me for those wheels and wagon parts," he called through the back as they rolled away.

They traveled down a long ridge, beyond the sound and smell of cattle, under the bright moon.

"Don't you want me to help out there?" Zeke kept asking, wanting to sit in the seat. "I'd be more help than Willard."

But Glass always said, "No, we'll make out. I want you back there taking care of your missus."

"There's some fellows following us," the boy said.

"How many?"

"Four, five. I think five. Every once in a while I catch a silvery shine."

Ellis Moffitt, one of Grand's 'scouts', was partial to silver conchos.

"You think they got anything in mind?"

"Like ambush?"

"Yes."

"There's no reason they'd want to harm us. Polly asked if I wanted an escort. Chance of Indians. Not a good chance but always a chance. They sometimes cross over beyond the forts and raid down here for horses."

"I know."

They traveled all night, and Glass slept for a while as the boy drove. The woman kept moaning, and her husband snored. Toward morning they dropped down into a deep, winding coulee and found water in a pothole. There were many antelope about. Glass turned the team over to Willard, mounted his saddle horse, which was on a lead string behind, and rode ahead to scout for a road. Once out of sight, he doubled back and climbed to some scabby-looking buttes, where he sat and watched the backtrail, wishing for a spyglass.

He saw nothing of the 'escort.' There was a chance they had made certain of his direction and turned back to report. Or they might have headed straight on to Casper and the pleasures it promised, using the trip only to get a couple of days in town.

He watched the country until the sun came up and shone warm on the rocks. His horse cropped the stiff yellow grass with regular ripping sounds. The sun grew warmer at his back, and he slept. He woke up startled and thought someone was coming up the slope directly onto him. There was movement but far, far away — two horsemen riding steadily northward. There was no telling who they were. An early heat had begun to radiate from the ground, distorting them so that they looked forty feet high. Apparently the pair had decided to go on to Casper, while the others turned back. He was sure Billy Grand would not give up a trip to Casper, so he was one of them. The other was probably Lejune. Despite the distance there seemed to be something in the long, dark figure recognizable as Lejune.

He rode ridges, came down declivities of crumbling clay, crossed dry watercourses one after another, and rode in narrow badlands coulees where white dirt and stone reflected the sun until there was not a shadow anywhere. Glare-heat came from the ground and the cliffs to shine bright on the underbrim of his hat. At a meeting place of many coulees, where a few box elder trees grew stunted and gnarled, he saw the wagon.

"We didn't know if this was the right

road," said the kid.

"Find any road in this country, it's the right one."

Some bright green along the base of a hillside attracted them. The horses could smell moisture. Although the surface was baked dry, a foot of digging turned soil that could be formed into damp balls, and at two feet the hole began to fill with water. It was muddy, it settled and had a good taste, and was very cold.

They rested and drove on, the coulee winding out and broadening to form a glaring white alkali sink. A wagon train was as clearly visible across the level ground. They drove and drove, and it disappeared, vanishing without a trace, and without a hoof or wheel mark on the ground.

"It was a ghost train," said Mrs. Pattison. "It's a portent of death. It is written that on the day of judgment strange sights and sounds will rise to confront the beholder, and the earth will open up to let out its dead."

"Ma'am, that was just a mirage. These white alkali sinks are famed for their mirages."

But she was insistent that the wagon train was a spirit manifestation, no doubt the ghosts of wagons, horses, and men vanished in seasons past.

"We'll never make it," she kept saying. "I'll never see a town again in this world."

"Well, the Lord's will be done," Zeke kept saying.

"If I die, I don't want to be buried out in this awful emptiness."

"You got to take the bitter with the sweet, Maw. That's how it goes. The Lord giveth and the Lord taketh away."

She wept. "Oh, no, no, no, I don't want to be laid away out here where it's so empty and forgotten. If I pass away, I want you to promise you'll take me back to the burying ground at Sallust."

"That'd be hard to do, Maw. Nebraska is a long way away. Of

course, I might be able to have you embalmed. Yes, I could! We got the money now. We could afford it. So you just rest easy. If you die, I'll get you in to Casper and if they have an undertaker there, I'll see to it you're embalmed."

Glass said to the boy, "You go back and talk to her. Send your paw up here to drive. He's not comforting her at all. Tell her she's going to get all right. Because she is. People don't generally die of the gallstones — they just wish they were dead."

Fort Casper was farther than he expected, and he came into it with a very tired team after midnight. There was a large wagon camp at one of the approaches to town and a couple of saloons were still open, but only the dregs of business — a poker game in the back of one, a lone light over the table, and two men at the bar in the other.

"Is there a doctor in town? I got a sick woman outside," Glass said,

126

entering the second saloon.

"Doc Stevens moved down to Rock Springs, but there's a surgeon at the post. You won't get in there until they blow the bugle. Sunup."

"Whyn't you take her to the hospital?"

"Is there one?"

"It's Mrs. Semple's. She's a nurse."

They found the house and got Mrs. Pattison inside. Afterward, feeling peculiarly set free, Glass spent some time just sitting, enjoying the coolness and the silence. At last he found the public stables, put his horses up, and went to bed in the hay.

14

Jim Bridger's Partner

IT had been a great wagonyard in the great days of the Oregon Trail, but of late years it had fallen into disrepair, the roofs gone from many of the sheds that had given shelter to families and their draft stock, and weeds growing up in many of the old corrals. In one large building a wagon foundry had been a booming enterprise, with the facilities for casting iron, setting tires, or making wheels entire, in fact able to build a wagon from endgate to tongue or, as people liked to say it, 'to junk three wagons and get four.' However, the great days had passed. There was the portion that had become a common livery barn, and only a blacksmith and his helper held down the repair shop. Three-fourths of the business had been taken by the railroad to the south. Even the gold camp traffic to Montana, which had been the hope of the town, had mostly gone south along the Overland and thence up the Salt Lake-Bannack trail or else cut off at Labonte creek to make the run across Indian country on the Bozeman road. Only the railroad projected to Montana via Wind River Canyon and the Big Horn kept hopes alive, and of course there was the army post. If the army ever pulled out, it was predicted, Casper would become a ghost town.

"Bridger?" said the blacksmith, putting his hammer down and turning to look at Leo Glass, who stood in the wide, smoky wagon entrance. "Jim Bridger?"

"I was told he was here."

"I don't know who told you that, mister. He's retired from the business and went home to Missouri. Parsons is taking care of his affairs, and then there are the railroad promotors."

"Which railroad?" He had heard of

about half a dozen.

"The Missouri, Bridger, and Northern. I had some literature on it. This is going to be a town of twenty thousand. They're dividing all that pasture into city lots. You can see the flags."

"Is the road open?"

"You mean the railroad?"

"I mean the Bridger wagon road. I got a trail herd and some wagons for Montana."

"Oh, of course. You can see Parsons. As I say, he's resident manager."

He walked through buildings, deserted except for a family of half-breeds, and saw the large sign reading,

BRIDGER ROAD CO. LTD
James Bridger
E. V. Parsons

Parsons proved to be a tall, lean, tough-faced man of forty. He was famed as a trapper, guide, and army scout. He had lost all except the forefinger and thumb of his right hand, so he shook hands with his left. He had been cooking his own breakfast. There were dribbles of pancake batter on his pants. The room was hot and filled with griddle smoke.

"Have you et your breakfast?" he asked.

"Yes, but I can eat another."

"It's the thing to do. Always eat twice if you got a chance because there'll come a time when you need a meal in reserve."

Frying pancakes and bacon and pouring big cupfuls of coffee black as licorice, he listened to Glass, inquired about the numbers of cattle and the extra horses, whether there were any ox teams, and how many of the travelers were women and kids under twelve.

"Of course I'll guide you to Montana," he said, sitting down to eat. "I been doing nothing here but sitting around hating myself. The goddamned railroads are ruining the country. I wish they'd never built the railroad. It used to be we got big outfits in here, eighty or ninety wagons, hundreds of oxen and horses, the wagon freight outfits, and the pony express. We had a coach company that competed with the Overland. Men with money, ten, twenty thousand tied up in stock and equipment. And all the people working for them. It took a year from spring to autumn to get to the Pacific, and now they do it in a week. They're filling the country up and spoiling it. Only one real frontier left and that's to the north. Canada. The only place left where you can stand on a river and wonder where it came from. Or Montana. All the same thing. Up north of the Mullan Road and the Missouri River just mountains and ranges of mountains to the end of the world. You climb one, and there's another and another, and you never reach the end of them. Jay Cooke has a railroad to go through there, but he'll never build it. It'd cost more money to drill through those mountains and hang trestle on the canyons than there is in the world. The Rothschilds or nobody else could do it. Bridger and me, we got the only practical route to Montana. The shortest and the best. But I'm sick of sitting here waiting for him. He knows a lot of people in the army, but they aren't going to help. You have to go where the money is. That's why I'd like to get up in Montana. They're digging it out of the ground fast as the government can mint to coin. And now the silver, too. Mountains of silver bigger than the Comstock. Will be when they get a railroad to haul the equipment. This office here — I haven't sold a share of stock all summer. Not a city lot, either. I'd be damned glad to guide you up to Montana and go shares on the fee. That is, I'll gamble double or nothing on you getting there — that's the confidence I have in our road."

There was a schedule on the wall. THE BRIDGER AND ROCKY MOUNTAIN EXPRESS WAGON ROAD AND TELEGRAPH CO. The tolls for each fifty-mile segment of the road were listed at : Wagon and 1 team, $2; Odd team, ea. $1; Man and horse $1; Cow or pack animal, 25c. At an estimated 450 miles to Bozeman City, the cost would run more than $3,000 for the entire outfit, and at double or nothing, $6,000.

"I'm afraid you're a trifle out of our class."

"Don't pay any attention to that. Who in hell could collect two bits for a cow? Or that dollar for a man and horse? They don't need a road. How could you force them to a toll gate? That schedule was just to prove to people with money to invest how profitable a road would be when and if. You can't make a cent out of emigrants. The only money would be made from freight and coaches. I'll guide you up the road for seven hundred dollars, and that's everything — the complete service, all the water and grass your stock can use along the way. I'll need a deposit."

He asked for $100, but all Glass had was a $20 gold piece. Instead he left his team and wagon, which was worth considerably more, Parsons promising to have one of his own men drive it and to meet him with a guide crew.

"I use breeds, not because they're the cheapest, but because they're the best. They're lazy at white man's work but plenty damn good in the country. They know how to avoid trouble, and you can't starve one the way you can a white man. Now, you can't drive down the Platte. Not with cattle. You'll lose half your herd in quicksand. The river's always off toward one bank or the other, and when they wade over, they're into it. You say this Broadbaker outfit is going to the Popo Agie? Then, they'll cross the Sweetwater and the old road. But if I was to split the herd, I'd pick the Platte crossing. Especially since you seem to think you'll have a row. Who is this Broadbaker? is that the man-eater? He'll have his hands filled over on the Popo because the government has bought off Chief

Washakie with that land. He'll have to fight Injuns and the army both to stay there, but maybe he has the force to handle 'em. Bring in enough settlers and they move the Injuns out every time. I think you're being real smart to head for Montana."

He found a map that had been printed as part of the railroad promotion, oversimplified with the Bridger Road shaded in to look like the great highway of the West, and he penciled in some landmarks.

"Don't pay attention to this map. This was got out to sell stock. It's one of the reasons Bridger got a reputation for being one of the worst liars in the West. Turn here and come northwest this side of the old Devil's Gate. It comes right along the mountains and it'll be rougher than hell, but wagons can make it. You may have to use a squaw winch on some of the coulees and gulches, but you'll make it and save yourself two or three days travel over coming anywhere close to Casper.

I'll meet you here at Teakettle Rock. I'll be there eight days hence, and unless I miss badly, you'll be there, too. It'll be just about traveling time for those cattle."

15

Meeting with a Gunman

GLASS had a look at his team, which he was leaving with Parsons, as a deposit, and at his saddle horse. Particularly at the saddle horse because he would be riding him back with very little rest. He had the livery man give him a bucket of oats at $1.00 per bucket.

"That's costlier feed than lots of men are getting these days," he said, staying around to see he got full measure.

"A good horse is worth more than most men, too," was the liveryman's answer.

He decided to walk over to see how Mrs. Pattison was faring. On his way he glimpsed the familiar figure of Billy Grand up the street.

Glass put off seeing about Mrs.

Pattison and walked at an easy gait, tall and watching for Grand. Billy had stepped behind some loaded freight wagons near the Miller Hardware platform and should have reappeared but he didn't. He walked to the end of the street and back without seeing him.

It was a suspicious way for him to act. He wondered if he had been sent to spy on him, or if he had instructions maybe to ambush him on the way back. The smart thing would be to go straight to the barn, saddle up, and start south for the herd. He could be miles away before Billy realized it, and hard to intercept. But a perversity that was part of his nature left him where he was. He didn't intend to run from Billy Grand. So he went to the hospital, inquired, and learned that the surgeon had come and left some medicine, and the woman was sleeping. With this hopeful news he walked down the street to a saloon called The Kansas House, just across from Miller's, and Billy was there. It was Moffitt with him rather than Lejune, as he had once supposed.

"Hello, Billy," he said. "I heard you were in town."

Moffitt had seen him an instant before, so Grand was able to look around in a perfectly composed manner, but Leo knew he was annoyed, that he had stayed in the upper end of town to avoid him, and that this somehow upset things.

"Who said I was in town? It was that kid, wasn't it?"

"Young Pattison? No. What the hell, Billy, didn't you expect to be recognized? Why, your fame has gone far and wide. All I been hearing from one end of the city to the other was how Billy Grand the gunman was here."

Grand looked rather pleased. He glanced at himself in the mirror. He could not help seeing how dashing and handsome he was. He was shorter than the other fellows, but he was the man whose 'pistols were swifter than weasels in a henhouse,' as the editor of the Wichita Globe had said, a fact that rendered the six-feet-one of Leo Glass of little importance.

Glass said, "If I'd known you were coming to Casper, you could have ridden along with us. We'd have been one happy family."

"With that old woman howling about her gallstones? No, thank you."

"You leave the trail herd, Billy? I mean, it's none of my affair, but Broad didn't say a word about it."

"No, I was sent as an escort. Lady's request. Polly. Didn't she say anything?"

"She mentioned you, Billy."

"Don't get the idea we were here hiding from you. We just didn't want to get close to that stinking, howling gallstone woman."

"She wasn't asking for you, either."

"You going to leave 'em here?"

"Yep."

"So now we'll only have the coyotes to howl. Do you want a drink?"

Leo had a drink and bought and remarked, "If you just came here to escort me and the sick woman, I'd imagine we might as well move along back. Are you ready to go?" He asked it on a hunch.

"No." He had Billy cornered. "You go along, and we'll catch up."

"I wouldn't think of it. It wouldn't be sociable. I'm going to go right along with you." He'd as willingly have traveled in the company of rattlesnakes.

"There's no need of that. We'll catch up. There's some work I got to have done. My horse. Loose shoe."

"I'm good with shoes. Let me have a look at him."

"The blacksmith's having a look at him."

"I was just at the blacksmith's."

"What in hell is this, a cross-examination? You think you're a lawyer or something?"

"Cross-examination? Why, Billy, what are you talking about?"

"All your goddamn questions. You

act like you doubted my word."

"All I said was — "

"I heard what you said."

They had attracted some attention. Grand's face had colored under the tan, and when angered, he had the voice of an excited boy. Men called him the 'kid killer,' but he was not so young, really. Perhaps twenty-four. Moffitt laid a hand on his arm, and he jerked away. "What the hell are *you* doing?" he snapped.

"Nothing," said Moffitt.

"We're all in this together," said Leo.

"No, we're not in anything together. We just got you safe into town. We were supposed to escort the woman, not you. Do I have to write it down on a piece of paper? There's nothing wrong with my horse, but" — something just came to him — "well, Ellis and I have a little private business to transact. We got a couple of women, if you want to know. Two's a pair, and two pair is two pair, and one extra is a full house. You understand how it is, Leo. After all, you got that girl, whatever her name is, back at the outfit. At least I think you do. She seems to follow you every time you ride out."

He thought that nothing Grand could say would anger him. He had set his mind to it. But unaccountably this did.

"You spread any of your dirty — " He stopped.

"What?"

"Never mind."

"No, you go ahead with what you started to say. My dirty what?"

"Stop it, Billy," said Moffitt.

"No, I want to hear this. This sounded like some sort of proclamation. What was it?"

"If you meant something about Polly Arbogast, say Polly Arbogast."

"Billy!" said Moffit.

"It's all right, Ellis, I ain't going to kill him. He's perfectly safe. No, I wouldn't mention her name. I'll leave that between you and Broadbaker."

Glass started for the door, and Grand called, "Leo! When you look behind you, that won't be me. If I want to kill you, I'll do it to your face."

"Will you, Billy?"

It took quite a while for the tingle of anger to leave him as he walked down the street.

He was standing in the stable waiting to have his horse saddled, a service accorded people who bought oats at a dollar a bucket, when a familiar figure appeared in the wide doorway. It was the Pattison kid.

"Hello, Will. How's your maw by this time?"

"She's slept and slept. The surgeon came back once. He thinks maybe if she lays quiet for a couple of weeks, she may be all right. On the other hand, he may have to take her over to the infirmary. What do they do to folks there, Mr. Glass?"

"I'll tell you what they do, Billy. They do the same thing with those gallstones that they do with arrowheads — they whack them out."

"Ain't it any worse than that?"

"I don't think so. Not if you know how."

He looked relived. "That being the case, I wouldn't mind leaving so much."

"You going somewhere?"

"I was in hopes I could go back with you."

"I've only got my saddle horse."

"How about the team?"

"I'm leaving the team and wagon as a deposit with Parsons."

"Oh." He sounded drearily disappointed. "Well, I guess you wouldn't let me walk behind?"

"It'd be too far."

"Yah."

"You better stay here with your folks."

He looked so beaten and forlorn standing in his ruptured boots, his old lid-top hat, and his patched rags that Glass took him up the street to a store and bought him a new outfit, spending most of his $20, and then giving him the change.

"No I couldn't take it."

"Yes, you can Will. You're on my payroll. I want you to help Mr. Parsons with the team. You tell him you're my driver. You tell him you can go along to Teakettle Rock. If your folks say it's all right that is."

"Oh it'll be all right. Why Paw wouldn't even *let* me turn down a steady job."

"Then that settles it. The first thing I want you to do is walk over and see E. V. Parsons. His office is at the wagon foundry. Tell him I'm just as willing it doesn't get out I've hired him or where he's to meet us."

"You mean at Teakettle? Should I tell him I'm working for you?"

"Yes and you tell him that."

"I'm hired all the way to Montana ain't I? I'll work cheap."

"Yes you are Will. I'll pay you ten dollars a month and found. You can be ramrod here on the North Platte."

"What's a ramrod Mr. Glass?"

"It's sort of a foreman on the way up."

It was a terrible thing to do to the Pattisons but the look of joy on the boy's face was a thing to remember.

"Be waiting for you at Teakettle, boss," called young Will.

"Take good care of the horses teamster."

"I'll keep 'em curried and grease the wagon."

16

The Ordeal of Willard Pattison

WHEN Leo Glass had become a lone horseman far across the flats and too far to wave to, Willard Pattison decided to go over to the hospital so his father could see him in his new clothes. The old man had been rough on him particularly of late, blaming him whenever something got broken or lost or when they caught him daydreaming instead of tending to business. At such times he was likely to come up without saying a word and whop him good. Willard still had a mark on him where his father had hit him with the hame strap. Also, his folks were always ragging him about how worthless he was when compared with Linton and Maxwell, his two older brothers, who had stayed to work in

Nebraska; how they had been out and earning when they were ten or eleven years old, and how he was the only Pattison to be low-down shiftless and lazy. Seeing him in the new duds with a steady job would make them sing a new tune.

On his way to the hospital, however, he met the man who had sold him the clothes, a Mr. Greenberg, who said to come along, then took him to a barber shop where he gave the man 50c out of his own pocket and told him to cut the boy's hair. After that the hat didn't fit, so Greenberg took him to the store and put a lampwick inside the sweatband and said that Willard could take it out again when he grew a new crop and sort of expand and contract with the season.

After the haircut the back of his neck felt cool and naked with prickly hairlike whiskers. It seemed as if cutting the hair had made him a good ten pounds lighter, although it had actually been only a couple of inches long at the back and less than that where Paw had got at him with the sheep shears. He walked along the street, bending this way and that and listening to the clump of his new boots — when he saw somebody that stopped him scared in his tracks. It was Billy Grand, and with him was that mean, big-jawed Ellis Moffitt. And oh, God, he hadn't got to Mr. Parsons with the message!

Grand and Moffitt were probably two of the so-called escort they had sighted coming to town. He wondered whether the others had come to town or whether they were waiting out in a blind coulee someplace to ambush Glass. He could larrup after him, but he was too far away. A whole hour had gone by. Then he thought it was probably all right because Glass, to intercept the herd, had taken a different route. Anyhow, he comforted himself, Glass was real smart and wary. He was cautious and knowing as a wolf.

Grand and Moffitt walked right past him. They didn't know who he was in the new duds. So he stood around and looked in the windows until they were safely down the street. Then he hurried between a couple of buildings to a back road and stayed behind woodsheds and ice-houses, tramping over the ash and bottle heaps in his new boots to get to the wagon foundry, but Grand and Moffitt had got their horses and were riding off ahead of him. He knew as sure as anything they were headed for Parsons'.

He didn't know what to do. Glass had left him with a job, and he had fooled around, showing his clothes off and letting the man buy him a haircut, and now it was too late. He wished he were dead. He wished he was dead and floating in the river, face down and eaten up by catfish so nobody would know who he was, ever. His pleasure of just a short while ago had turned to misery and ashes. He couldn't imagine ever liking the clothes again. Or anything.

The wagon works was located beyond

the edge of town. There was nothing to hide behind except some eaten-off sage, so he had to lie low and just watch, anguished and helpless, while Grand and Moffitt covered the distance. But as soon as they were out of sight, he ran as hard as he could coming up from the river side, through some corrals and old, pole-roofed sheds, getting there almost as soon as they did. He sneaked up and heard Moffitt say something. They were walking. He could hear the jingle of their spurs. One of them rapped on a door. A voice answered, saying to come in, and the door closed. He peeked and saw a sign reading BRIDGER ROAD CO. LTD. The door was only a frame with cheesecloth over it to keep out the flies. He wanted to creep up and listen, but he didn't dare. He thought of climbing up on the roof and listening at the stovepipe and he thought of sneaking in the back door and finally he got around to the other side and listened at a window.

A voice spoke very close. It must

have been Parsons saying, "Well, that may be, but it doesn't change things any." Then Grand said something, very soft-voiced. His voice reminded Willard of warm liver. He was telling Parsons how they had just ridden into town and missed Leo Glass, darn the luck, and that it was going to cause everybody a lot of bother because Leo was supposed to do this and that and get supplies, but he supposed if Bridger & Parsons wouldn't trust him with the plans, then he'd just have to make out somehow.

"You're jumping to a conclusion, aren't you?" Parsons said quite loud.

"Like what?"

"Like we had any *plans*."

"You have, haven't you?" Billy asked, losing some of his warm-liver tone.

"As far as that's concerned, how do you know he came here at all?"

"We heard he did. They told us."

"Who told you?"

"I don't know the fellow's name. Right down the street."

"You bring that fellow around. I'd

like to talk to him."

"Are you trying to tell us we're liars, mister?" Moffitt asked.

"I wouldn't go to the bother of calling you anything."

"What do you mean by that?"

"Get out of my place," said Parsons.

"Now, let's calm down and be friends." It was Grand with his voice like liver again. "Do you deny — "

"I don't need to deny anything."

"All right, Mr. Parsons, if you say — "

"I said *get out*. This is my business, and I'll run it without your advice."

There was a clumping as the men left and a slap of the front door. Willard could see their shadows out front and hear them talking. He sneaked around the buildings. Somehow he couldn't find the same route he had followed in coming. He was inside a shed with the sun in slits through the pole roof and the front all open. He could hear them again. They seemed to be riding that way. He could even hear the jinglebob affair that Moffitt had on his bit chain.

There wasn't time to get out through the back of the shed. All he could do was stop where he was, not move, not even breathe — and hope. If you did that, people would sometimes walk right past you. Even antelope would walk past you if the wind was right.

"I doubt Glass would tell him one way or the other," Billy Grand was saying.

"The team and wagon was there."

"It doesn't mean anything. He might have left it for the gallstone woman."

Then they stopped talking. It was very baffling. He couldn't hear their voices or the hoofs or bridle chain or anything. He started to creep out away from the wall, his head up, looking this way and that. He had decided to risk taking a peek out front, when suddenly there was Billy Grand, standing with a gun in his hand. They had left their horses and walked. Billy was in front, and Moffit was around back.

"Well, look what we got here!" said Billy.

He wanted to run, but he was too scared. His legs felt dead. He stood feeling sick enough to throw up, while Moffitt came through the back door.

"Good God, Ellis, look at this! He's gone and got himself a whole new outfit. Ain't he the dandy. He's a regular dude. Where'd you get money for all these duds? Is this how you spent all that money they took up in the collection for your maw?" When Will couldn't answer, his throat being so tight, Grand shoved him into the wall. "How about it, kid? Is that how our money was spent?"

"No! It was bought for me!"

"Who by?"

"Leo Glass!"

"Well, I'll be damned. Let's see the hat."

He whipped it off Will's head and looked at it inside and out. "It's kind of stiff, ain't it? Maybe we ought to beat it out a little. You're supposed to whop a new hat on your leg like this. If we just had some water, now. Or some good old horse manure would do."

"Leave that alone!"

"What's that? What you say?"

Will tried to get the hat back, but Grand held it out of his reach and poked him him in the stomach with his .45.

"What was that you were saying?"

"Nothing."

"Ellis, he's got to be a pretty uppity fellow since he got the new clothes. He's ordering folks around."

"What do you want with me?" Will cried.

"You quiet down. Now, we want some straight talk from you. How come he bought you this fancy outfit?"

"I don't know."

"Empty out your pockets."

He did, spilling coins, washers, bits of kid treasure he'd picked up, and an old jackknife.

"Where'd you get that money?"

"It's mine."

"I know, but where'd you get it? That's a lot of money for a wagon kid like you. Did you steal it from your maw?"

"No, Glass give it to me."

"Why?"

"It's my pay. I'm working for him."

"The hell you are. Do you hear that, Ellis? He's working for him."

"Doing what?" asked Moffitt.

"Just . . . "

"Doing what?" he demanded, ready to slap him down.

"Hold on, Ellis." He placed his boot inside the hat and pulled it out of shape as Will watched in anguished silence. "How about it? Tell me what you're doing for him, or would you rather I shoved my foot through this hat?"

"Just sort of taking care of things. Watching the team and wagon."

"Until when?"

"Until I don't know. Until he calls for them."

"What was he planning with Parsons?"

"I don't know."

"You know, all right."

"I didn't even know he'd been to Parsons."

"Why were you sneaking around here, then?"

"I don't know."

"You don't know anything, do you?" He had put his gun away while working on the hat. Now he dropped the hat on the ground, clamped his boot on it, and drew the gun again. He cocked it, and while the kid's knees buckled with fear he pressed the muzzle under his ear. "Now, you give me some straight answers, or I'm going to pull this trigger."

Young Willard Pattison might have answered if he could have, but in terror all he could do was whimper. The whimper came in with a rapid tremolo of sobs. He began to shake out of control. He might have fallen if Moffitt had not grabbed him from behind.

"Out with it!"

"I don't know, I don't know . . . "

Both men were silent. A door had closed. It was Parsons. He walked, clomping, over some boards. The house was only a stone's throw away. Parsons could see the horses but not the men. He walked on, his boots fading along the cinder path. Both men were turned to listen. Moffitt had relaxed his hold. Billy's gun was not pointed . . .

Will let himself go limp and he fell. He was free and crawling along the ground. He jumped up to run, but Moffitt got in front of him. He dodged back and forth like a cornered rabbit. He started to yell "Mr. Parsons!" and Moffitt smashed him backhand to the ground. He tried to roll over and dive between their feet. Moffitt kicked him. It got him alongside the head. He sat with ears ringing and blackness across his eyeballs, trying to yell, but not a sound would come from his throat. Moffitt had him by the collar. He couldn't breathe. He clawed and fought while Moffitt cursed him in a raw whisper and slammed him again and again against the wall. When consciousness came back, the men didn't seem to be worried anymore.

"Where's your horse? Do you have a horse?" Billy was asking him.

"No."

"We can walk him between us," said Moffitt.

"In them new boots?" And they laughed.

"Where's my hat?" Will sobbed.

It had been walked on. Billy picked it up. "Are you real sure this is your hat? Somehow it don't look at all like the one you generally wear. It ain't got your style. I think we ought to fix that."

While Will watched, not daring to make a sound, Billy took out his jackknife, stropped the blade on his pants, and cut the crown all around except for a piece of felt about two inches wide on one side.

"There!" he said. "See how it works? You can get some air in it and cool your brains off. Now what? How'd you like to have your new boots ventilated?"

He did not know what the word ventilated meant.

"Answer me."

"Huh?"

"Let's get him away from here," said Moffitt.

"All right, kid, let's go."

"Where you taking me?"

"You really want to know? We're going to take you out of town where nobody can hear the shot and kill you."

He was so frightened that his legs were dead. He kept falling when he tried to walk. They got him between their horses and kept him walking between them. Moffitt held onto his collar, and every time he sagged or moved wrong Moffitt almost strangled him.

"It ain't so bad to get shot in the back of the head, do you think, Ellis? I don't think so. You don't even know it's happened. There's a joint right along the sides of a persons's skull, and if you put a bullet just right, it will come off like the lid of a sugar bowl. It's true. We can fix you up so your folks will think you've been scalped by Indians."

"Scalped deep."

"Ya!"

Will kept stepping on sagebrush and grass bumps. His boots were stiff, making him stumble. They stopped out in the sagebrush and asked him again what the plans were. Then they walked again and asked him again and finally they took him down a little coulee and told him that this was the place.

"We didn't want to do this, you know, kid, but you didn't leave us any choice," said Grand. "Now, I'm going to give you just fifteen seconds. You tell us before fifteen seconds is up and you can live." And he pulled out a watch.

If I do tell, they'll kill me anyhow, his mind cried out, suddenly working at top speed. But they won't kill me as long as there's a chance of finding out. When I tried to run, they hit me, and I didn't know anything. If they hit me this time, maybe I'll be knocked out cold. He had seen a man brought in unconscious after being thrown from a horse, and it was like he was asleep for a day and a night. Then suddenly he roused up, little the worse, and drank a quart of water. What Will hoped was that something like that would happen to him.

Without warning he broke and ran. He ran up the coulee over cactus and sagebrush, through the dirt and gravel, and he heard them galloping behind him. He was wrapped around the throat by a quirt. The pain was like white fire. He clawed to free himself and he felt as if the ground had been jerked from under his feet. As he lay there it seemed that a horse was tromping right over him. He tried to roll over and get up. He made it as far as his hand and knees. A man was down kicking him. It was Billy Grand kicking him in the side of his head. He felt himself being kicked and kicked and kicked, each time with a clubbing impact that drove him a bit further toward the edge of blackness. He tried to shout out, and it was like a cry at a great distance, uttered by someone else, fading, fading . . .

17

Bullet in the Back

ANDY BROADBAKER was a light sleeper and with the first tremble of weight on the steps leading up to his wagon he came awake.

"Who is it?" he asked, swinging his feet to the floor. He slept with a pistol on the floor within reach. He didn't pick it up, but in the dark he could feel its solid metal against the side of his foot.

"Me."

It was the voice of Billy Grand. Broadbaker had been expecting him. Glass had returned in the afternoon, and Grand ought to have found out all there was to know in an hour or two and followed him. They should have come back at almost the same time. But they could not resist having a few drinks at one of the bars. Billy was not exactly trustworthy, but he had other qualities that made up for it. When you hire men for special jobs, you always have to make allowances. Moffitt was more solid and dependable, but he was the type to hesitate at the ultimate moment and be killed. The two made a good team.

"All right, come on in."

Billy Grand would have been interested to know that Broadbaker had his gun in his hand when the door opened. He was a naturally well prepared man. He had an idea — nothing reasoned out, just an impression — that someday he would have to kill Billy Grand.

"I can't see a thing."

"That's all right. How did it go?"

"Well, it didn't."

"What do you mean?"

"He was in visiting Parsons at the road company office, but Parsons wouldn't tell us much. Glass left his team and wagon but maybe for the Pattisons. He hired the Pattison kid, I don't know what for. Did he get back yet?"

"Yes, hours ago. Where were you?"

"It ought to be pretty plain where we were. We were in town inquiring around. It takes time."

"What did the kid say? The Pattison kid?"

"Nothing."

"Nothing! You let it go at that?"

"No, we brought him back with us."

"Where is he?"

"Out in the dark. Ellis has got him."

"You mean he came all this way and wouldn't say a word? He must have had some kind of a story."

"Well, he wasn't in the shape to talk. It was an accident. He made a run for it, and we hit him too hard."

"And you brought him back here! That was an idiotic thing to do. You know what I have to contend with,

with them." He indicated the Arbogast camp.

"Well, we couldn't leave him and we had to come back ourselves. What did you expect us to do? The only thing left was to kill him."

"That's what we'll have to do anyhow. We can't risk having him on the loose with his blatting mouth."

Billy Grand sounded annoyed — all the effort he'd made and no appreciation for it! "All right, I'll go out and kill him right now."

"No, let me talk to him." He got dressed and went outside. It was a little past midnight. The cattle had a tense unease. The night was unusually warm, and you felt that a spark might ignite something, like powder in the pan of an old flintlock. There were no clouds, but there was something electric in the air. The cattle were tired, there had been a series of camps with never enough water, they filled up on a thin mud and bawled all night and day, and no matter how early the camp broke, a few were up and moving.

"Did you talk to Glass?" asked Billy.

"No."

"Where's he sleeping, now that he gave his outfit away?"

"Who?" He was preoccupied and annoyed.

"Glass."

"I don't know. That's his cart."

"*His* cart?"

"Lon Arbogast gave it to him," Broadbaker said with a touch of bitterness.

"The old fellow's always up and stirring. You know — Dad what's-his-name."

"Dad Haze."

"Yes. He goes to bed one place and next morning he comes from another. It's like he expected somebody to shoot him in the night."

"Well, that's how it is. The older you get, the more you want to live."

Nobody was bedded down very close. Broadbaker's wagon set out in the open, fifty yards or so from the cookwagon

171

and at least that far from the Arbogast camp. The moon kept passing under clouds and coming out bright again. After walking for about an eighth of a mile, they came to Grand's horse, tied to some large sage. They walked on. The herd was left to one side. It became very quiet. They came to an area of shallow gullies.

"Ellis?" Grand called.

"Yah?"

He was standing with a couple of horses, and the Pattison kid was sitting on the ground.

"I had to buy that horse," said Billy. "He's a terrible muley, but he cost me twenty-five dollars."

It had probably cost about fifteen.

"Do you have a bill of sale?" Broadbaker asked.

"No! If a man can't take a fellow's word for — "

"All right." He called to the kid. "You! Come here."

The kid looked different. Somebody had cut off most of his hair. He had different clothes. He didn't want to move, and Moffitt shoved and booted him. He tripped and fell down and lay staring at Broadbaker.

"You better tell me what Glass is figuring on, Willard," he said, "because I'm not going to waste much time with you."

The kid got to hands and knees. Sag-jawed, he looked up at him.

"Well?" barked Broadbaker.

"I don't know. I don't know anything."

"Of course he doesn't know anything," Broadbaker said, turning on Grand. "Why would anybody tell him anything?"

"He had him hired."

"I have you hired, too."

"Can I go? Can I?" whimpered Will.

"Yah, you can go." He nodded to Billy. The kid suddenly realized what they intended and ran. Billy drew his gun. He seemed to heft its balance. Then he brought it up quickly to aim and he pulled the trigger. The gun came to life with a crash and lash of flame. The kid was running full speed. There was some heavy sage up the side of the draw, and he was making for it. At the final second, slowed by the steepness, he turned and started down. But it did not cause Billy Grand to miss. The bullet hit him, and he went forward with both hands lifted shoulder-high. He fell and slid face down.

Some nearby cattle were up and milling. A cowboy on night herd uttered an exclamation of surprise.

"Who fired that shot?" a second man asked, riding that way. It was the night boss, Clint Norden.

"I don't know."

"Who's that over there?" Norden asked, angry but not wanting to get any closer.

"Answer him," said Broadbaker. "Tell him it was an accident."

"Me?" asked Billy.

"Yes."

"Accident, Clint," he called.

"You get these critters to running,

and it's likely to be your last accident."

"Sorry."

After a while Norden and the cowboy rode away.

"Should we bury that kid?" asked Moffitt.

"Find him," said Broadbaker.

"He's in that deep sage."

"Find him, I said."

"Here's his blood. He bled like a hog."

"Do you see him?"

"Yes, he's down there in the bottom. On his face. Want me to put another through him?"

"Of course not. Come along, or Norden will be back here snooping."

"Does it bother you to kill a kid like that?" asked Moffitt when he was alone with Billy Grand.

"Does it bother you to butcher a yearling rather than a steer? One wagon kid more or less — what of it?"

"How many men you killed, Billy?"

"Counting this? Eleven."

"Gawd! Eleven!"

"It might have been a dozen. I'm not sure of one."

"What happens when you get to thirteen? That's an unlucky number."

"Especially if you happen to be the number thirteen! Let's get to bed, Ellis, or we won't have time to get up in the morning."

18

The Hat

"**W**HERE'D you get the hat, Pedro?" asked Leo Glass, coming from breakfast. In fact, he was riding with his usual breakfast of thick bacon and a triple roll of pancake in his hand.

Pedro looked like a Mexican, but he was actually a Montenegrin sailor who had jumped ship in San Francisco and drifted by one stage and another into cowboying. Everybody called him Pedro because of his resemblance to Pedro Sanchez, the villain in a popular play on the repertoire of the Maude Weston Stock Company. He had a new hat with the crown cut cleanly off except for a strip about two inches wide at the right side.

"Found it. Like a damper in a

stovepipe!" he said, showing his yellowish teeth and working the crown.

"Let me see that hat."

It was the same hat Glass had bought young Willard Pattison. He remembered the make, not one usual in the West but cheaper and with a gaudy brightness that a youngster would like. It had taken a tromping, and the crown had been cut cleanly, as if by a razor. A lampwick had been placed under the sweatband. He remembered nothing of that, but the fellow at the store might have put it in when he wasn't paying too much attention.

"Where'd you find this, Pedro?"

"Yours?"

"No. I think — well, it has me puzzled."

"Come along. I show you."

Pedro took off at a lope, and Leo followed. The wagons had all moved off, leaving the empty prairie. He stopped in heavy sage at the bottom of a small draw.

"Right here."

There were boot prints around and the tracks of horses and cattle.

"I'm going to keep this, Pedro. I think I know who it belongs to. Don't say anything, eh?"

"Sure! I say nothing."

It was the same hat, but how had it gotten there? Had Will followed him back to camp? Perhaps he wanted to warn him about something.

After Pedro was gone, he hunted all over the area, riding a mile down the draw and back and forth through all the deep sage, but there was nothing.

He noticed then that he was being watched. A rider had tarried behind the herd. He thought instantly of Grand, but it was not. It was Polly Arbogast.

"What's that you have?" There was a strange, tight note in her voice.

"A hat. Why? Did you ever see it before?"

"No." She took it and examined it. "I never saw it but I heard about it. Is it his — Will Pattison's?"

"Yes. Wait a minute. What do you

know about him?"

She did not answer. She was so nervous that he felt she didn't even hear his question. He could see that she was afraid someone was observing them. She did not know what to do with the hat. She rode away, motioning him to follow. Amid the sage and well out of view, she got down, twisted the hat into a tight roll, and hid it in a badger hole.

"Why'd you do that? Where is he? What happened last night?"

She motioned for him to come and rode away at a stiff gallop. She was light on a horse, weighing between ninety and a hundred pounds. It was a great advantage. Polly always seemed to be on the gallop, but she seldom wore out her horse. She got far ahead of Glass and in front of the herd. The Arbogast wagons were over to the north, and the one driven by Lon Arbogast the farthest of all. She came up beside him, and he stopped. They were talking when Glass rode up.

Lon, whose face was deeply creased for his thirty-five years, looked particularly taut this morning. He gripped the reins very hard. And he kept looking over the rise of country to the south.

"Goddammit!" he said to his sister. It was evident she had gone straight and done what she had promised not to.

"I tell you, he found the hat."

"Anyhow, stay on that side of the wagon."

She went in back and opened the endgate door. It was light inside, with the sun white through the canvas. A lot of stuff had been roped to the wagon box, and a bed was made on the floor. As Glass expected, there lay young Will.

"It's all right," she said. "It's Leo."

Willard Pattison, gaunt and staring, with a purple-bruised face, and further strange from the skinning the barber had given him, had raised himself to his elbows.

"Hello, Mr. Glass," he said. His lips

were cracked and so thick he could hardly use them. "They got up to Parsons' ahead of me — "

"It's all right, Will. I shouldn't ask you to stand against those fellows."

"I blowed the job."

"No, you didn't, Will. You did fine. You did better'n any man in this camp. You stood against 'em and came out alive. Now, you lie back down and get some rest. You'll be no good to me unless you do."

"But Parsons didn't tell 'em anything. Not a word. I was listening."

"You did a good job, Will."

He moved back while Polly, very light and quick on her feet, sprang inside to do some work around his bed.

"Hurry!" said her brother through the front opening. "His wagons are swinging over this way."

"Oh, the devil with him!"

But she hurried to get outside and make sure that the door and a blanket drape were both closed to keep anyone from seeing in. She was barely finished when Lon got the wagon rolling.

"How is he?" Glass asked him, staying beside.

"He's getting along all right. For having taken a pistol slug." Lon didn't want to talk. He was very nervous.

"Where?"

"It just seemed to have cracked some ribs. I don't think it hit anything vital. But it was like getting hit by a club. He couldn't even make sense for a while, but finally he got to talking about Grand. I don't know what the truth is. I'm not accusing anybody."

"Who found him?"

"Polly."

"When did she?"

"I don't know. It was dark. She heard them out there."

"*Them?*"

"You ask her about it, mister. I've got enough trouble without making any accusations."

He rode after her.

"Yes, I woke up and heard them. I

recognized his voice."

"Billy's?"

"And Andy's," she said reluctantly. "So you were right about him! He was everything you said."

"I'm not gloating."

"I laid there listening. I don't know why, but for some reason, Grand coming up in the middle of the night, and then there was something I could *feel* . . ."

"I understand."

"Then I heard the shot. That's when I got up. After a while they came back, the three of them, and with three horses. You see, I knew they'd gone away walking. So one of the horses had to be — you see?"

"Yah."

"Finally I couldn't stand it any longer, so I got up and went out there and I heard him moan. He was just sitting there. There was a low place where the prairie had washed out — he had fallen into it and was sitting there. Somebody had shot him in the back.

The bullet broke some ribs and tore his flesh, but it glanced and went on again. His clothes were just solid blood. All caked and stiff and full of dirt, but he wasn't bleeding any more. He couldn't tell me what had happened. He didn't seem to know. Why did they do it to him? Why?"

"I left him in town to take care of the team, and they must have got hold of him. I'd called at Bridger and Parsons'. When they couldn't learn anything from Parsons, they got hold of Will. They must have wanted to find out awfully bad. It really must be important — to do that to a kid."

"Everything Broadbaker has is tied up in this drive."

"But to — "

"I'm not excusing it, I'm just explaining it. He says it's sink or swim. The whole effect of a lifetime. It's important to us, too. So you can't blame Lonnie about not being happy. That kid in the wagon. If Broad rides up, it'll be worse than finding him with you or with Beer or Denison. It will make Lonnie look like a traitor. He can't fight Broadbaker like you or the rest. He's in no position to fight him. Yet, there's that kid in the wagon! Try to look at it his way."

"I am. We'll have to move him. If he could delay, fall away back, and then I'd have Kopke come around. He's got a good wagon and he's not afraid. I don't like him very well, but he's a tough Dutchman and — "

"No, we're not moving him at all!"

They rode together, leaving the herd behind. He was strongly aware of her presence. He did not look at her — he seemed to look far out across the land — but he did not miss any of her movements, the characteristic way in which she turned her head, tucked stray wisps of hair under her hat, her high manner of holding her chin, of turning her body at the waist when her attention was diverted this way or that. She was very slim, and yet her hips were broad, a form accentuated by her leather riding skirt with its three-buckle belt. Her coarse shirt made a strong contrast with her skin, which was smooth and soft beyond comprehension. He had lived in a land of men, and women had been the coarse creatures of the wagons or the bedraggled women of the camps, prematurely aged and turned either to pulpy flesh or skeleton by nightlife and whiskey. The girl beside him was a miracle. He had the feeling that any wrong move might make her vanish. Her perfection had the quality of illusion.

However, the illusion proved itself to be a very real thing of body, voice, and annoyance when she suddenly stopped and said, "Glass! Just wait a minute! Say what's on your mind. Are you afraid *I'll* go to Broadbaker?"

"No, of course not."

"Then, what about Parsons? What are your plans?"

"Parsons will have a guide party together, waiting for us at Teakettle Rock."

"Where's that?"

He pointed toward the place, an uncertain shimmer of blue mountain to the northwest.

"Is that the turnoff to the Big Horn?"

"Yes — Wind River Canyon, the Bridger Road."

She cried, "Why are you so stubborn?"

He looked at her in surprise. Her mouth was tight. He could see that her whole body was trembling from repression.

"Me, stubborn?" he said.

"Yes! You can't give in and go to the Popo Agie?"

"And leave Broadbaker the winner?"

"*Winner?* This isn't a ball game."

"I can't choose just like that, one way or the other. The wagoners won't follow me."

"I think they would. And it might be the best thing for them."

"No, and I'm not free to take my outfit just where I choose. Maybee had certain commitments. Foolish or not, I took those commitments over."

"Oh, Leo!" She turned to him. She needed him, and he wanted to do everything for her. He wanted to say yes, that he would go to the Popo. However, what he said had been true — the wagoners probably would vote against it.

She said, "Leo, for *me*. Do it for me, please."

"I'd do anything for you."

"The — "

"But you don't have to follow Broadbaker. Let him go his way. The Arbogasts can go theirs. You can come with us. That's what you'll have to do, Polly."

It seemed that this possibility had not previously occurred to her.

"No, we can't!" But she said it in a way that gave him hope.

"Why?"

"I don't know! Just we can't."

"Talk to Lonnie."

"After our promise — everything? No, no!"

"Well, what kind of a future will he

have? Is he going to enjoy being under that man's heel for the rest of his life? You've seen the hold Broadbaker has on him. Right now — " He was going to say that right now Lonnie was frightened pale for fear Broadbaker would come and find he had given help to the kid. And it wasn't a thing like being considered a traitor. It was just plain physical fear.

"I don't know, I don't know! I haven't any reason to think Lonnie would listen to me, anyhow."

"He'll by God listen to me!"

"No, let me talk to him. Where will you try to break away?"

"The North Fork."

"North Fork of the Plate?"

"Yes. It's the valley you see. And the hills backing it. We'll turn north-northeast."

"I don't know."

"Talk to him." He took hold of her, demanding an answer. "Will you talk to him?"

"Yes!"

"You tell him this is the time to stand up and fight for his life. Like his grandfather did when he stood up and made Arbogast the biggest name west of Omaha. You can't tell what kind of a man Lonnie Arbogast might be if he just once decided to stand up to Broadbaker! And it's not as if he wouldn't have some help!"

19

The Crossing at North Fork

GLASS said nothing about Willard Pattison in the emigrant camp. There were no spies, but the men and — at least one of the women — had friends among Broadbaker's cowboys. No clear lines were drawn at grub pile, and it was not unusual to see Wash Ditson or some other cowboy eating at one of the emigrant wagons, or McCoy or bachelor Ted Goings mooching from Frogs Braskin, their friend from down in the sandhills country. And so word of things always got around.

At a night meeting half a day's travel from the North Fork he outlined his plans. He said it looked as if the cattle would reach the North Fork about noon, day after tomorrow. He wanted the wagons, all possible, to be driven by the women and kids. The men should all be at the river, waiting to cut the stock. He had a list of all the brands. The herd would hit the river at a pretty good clip, thirsty, and they would spread out to drink. Broadbaker would have his men hard at it getting them across and watching them from the quicksand. He would see what was going on soon enough and probably try to stop it. However, they would show him a solid front. He wanted Brown, Kopke, Denison, and Old Dad to form a tough center. It would be their job to face Grand and his bunch.

"Where'll you be?" asked Beer.

"I'll try to be where I'm needed."

"By God, I got a simpler way. Why don't we just kill that man-eater? Kill him and be done with it."

"That's his way."

"All right, so it's his way. It means we have precedent to go on."

"Maybe you'd like the job, Archer," said McCoy.

"If you mean by that I'm a-feared of — "

"Never mind," said Glass. "There might not be a shot fired. It depends on the stand we make. Broadbaker may say *go and good riddance*."

"How about the Arbogasts?"

He knew by the tone and the waiting that his relationship with the Arbogasts had been the subject of talk.

"We'll wait and see. I don't think it's much of a secret that Lon Arbogast hates Broadbaker as much as any of us."

"You mean there's a chance of him joining?"

"I only said to wait and see. If he does be ready."

"I'll be ready for *that* one!" said Archer Beer derisively. "I'll also be ready for Kingdom Come and the skies raining bread and honey. Because when he gets the guts to stand against Broadbaker, the end of the world is at hand."

Later Glass walked to the Arbogast

wagon. He was stopped by the click of a gun hammer and a man appearing in the night. It was Lon, with his long-barreled deer rifle in his hands.

"Oh, it's you," he said, letting his rifle drop.

"How's the kid?"

"Asleep. He moves, and it hurts him, and he wakes up. He's asleep now, though. I gave him some laudanum."

"Has the wound started to swell? If it has, maybe we better have Brown look at it. He knows some about doctoring. He was an apothecary back in — "

"No, it's not swollen more than normal. He's doing all right. His wound is hot, but his forehead isn't. He isn't sweating too much, either. If he gets bad, I'll see you."

They would have to move him by tomorrow night, the last chance before North Fork. Unless Lon had decided to join them. He waited for him to say something, but he didn't, and after a while they said good night.

Polly was watching from the shadows

and she followed.

"What did he say? Is he joining up?"

"No. Did you mention it?"

"I wanted him to mention it."

"Does he know about the North Fork?"

"Yes." She touched his hand. "It's going to be all right. Everything is going to be all right. You'll see."

"Good night, Polly."

"Good night."

The morning dawned burning hot and cloudless. They traveled on and on with the valley of the North Fork always in sight but apparently getting no closer. As the day advanced and it would have been customary to let the herd slack off a little, Broadbaker had his men urging greater speed. A natural bed-ground lay on a stretch of grassy bench at the base of some hills. There were pines on the hills, brush in the gullies, and evidences of water not far away. The cookwagon, flying its red flag, had indeed driven that direction a swing of about three miles to the upcountry south, but a horseman rode over at a long gallop and after a while the cookwagon doubled sharply back and rolled northeast, avoiding grass and small streams, for no place imaginable except the North Fork. It was plain that Broadbaker had decided to make the crossing that night.

Denison, angry, came up to shout at Glass, "He's been warned!"

"Not necessarily."

"Then, why make the run tonight? He's damn near had these critters at a lope for the last two hours. He's been warned what our plans are."

"Who do you suspect?"

Denison was thinking of the Arbogasts. He wanted to say that Glass had fallen in love with the girl and told her what he shouldn't, but he restrained himself. "I'm making no accusations. But just the same, he's found out what our plans are."

"Put yourself in his place. He knows we'll try it someplace and where would we find a chance as good? He's smart and as wary as a wolf. Use your head, Dension. He doesn't need to be warned."

He rode back with Denison to his wagon and had a drink from the water keg. Other wagons came and stopped, and men on horseback.

"Yes, it's pretty plain he's going to cross over tonight," Glass said. "All right, then, we'll make our move, too. It's the full moon time, and we can work all night. We'll get over on the far side like we planned and start to cutting. We might as well settle it now."

He rode over where Polly was driving. He could see nothing of Lonnie. He had probably taken over one of the supply wagons. All their cowboys were on the drive.

He tied his horse to the back and climbed through to see the kid. He was skinny and weak, but he had no fever. Only the hotness from lying in the sun, which came through the canvas top.

"I feel good," said Will. "Only I'm getting awful tired of this jouncing. Fearful tired. Riding on my back. If I could get up and sit."

"Tomorrow, maybe. Have you eaten?"

"No, but I've drunk a bucket."

"Don't you get hungry at all?"

"I think I'll be hungry for supper."

Glass went up to stand behind Polly. "Broad is making it for the crossing tonight," he said.

"I know."

"How about Lonnie? What does he say?"

"He'll do it."

"Split off with us?"

"Yes."

But he knew she wasn't sure.

"Unless Broad gets hold of him. It isn't that he's afraid! Broad can just talk Lon into things!"

Glass left her and saddled a fresh horse, then he galloped down to the North Fork, where Frogs Braskin already had his cookwagon mired in sand. Point riders came up to help him with lariat tow ropes. By the time Glass was across, Old Dad, Kopke, Brown, and Denison were across to meet him. McCoy and his two sons arrived a minute later.

Al Manning rode over and saw them. "What in hell are you fellows doing," he bellowed, "waiting to get your pictures took?"

Nobody answered him. They waited on a grassy bank under the aspen trees, a strip of coolness and quiet before the cattle came.

"Do we start now?" asked Frye, getting there with his three riders.

"When the cattle come," said Glass. "You know the brands."

"I ought to. I've looked at 'em enough."

Glass called for the men and said, "Here's a couple more — the Tilted A and the Rafter 6."

"Those are Arbogast brands."

"Right."

"Gawd! Does Broadbaker know about this?"

"He will."

"What's going on here?" asked Al Manning.

"We're cutting out for Montana."

"You mean you've picked this time to cut the herd?"

"Yes."

"Like hell you'll cut the herd! We're going to get 'em over and beyond this quicksand and up on the flats. If you cut any herd, it will be tomorrow."

"We're cutting the herd, Al," said Glass, dismounting.

If there was fighting to be done, he wanted to do it from the ground. Al turned back without another word and recrossed the stream, having a hard time of it because of the front-running cattle. In about three minutes Billy Grand, Ellis Moffitt, and Grumbauer came over, almost abreast, and followed by Lejune, Axtell and the rest of the scouts. Frye was the first man they came to.

"What's this about you cutting the herd?" Grand asked.

"Those are my cattle," said Frye, "and I'll do what I want with them."

"They're part of the herd."

Grand swung down from his dripping horse. Frye didn't know what to do. He did not want to give in, but he knew that Grand might kill him.

"Drive your cattle, Frye!" said Glass. "I'll take care of this."

"Who the hell's giving orders?" said Billy Grand.

"You know how to read brand, Billy?"

"Yes, but brand doesn't mean a damn thing — "

"It does to us."

"Maybe I got a brand for you. In forty-five caliber."

"That's good talk, Billy. The secret is not to say it but do it. Or do you need a thirteen-year-old kid to do it to? Is that the kind of a gunman you are, Billy?"

Grand winced. Everyone was looking at him. He tired to carry it off with a jeer and a swagger. "What are you talking about? Say it right out, Glass."

"You picked on a thirteen-year-old kid and shot him in the back. I'm talking about Will Pattison. Oh, you're Brave Billy, the gunman."

Billy laughed and spat. Perhaps if the spit had not landed on Glass, it would have been different. It was stringy and it ran down the front of his shirt. Glass only laughed. Infuriated, Billy dropped the reins and sprang away from his horse. He landed in a spread-legged crouch, his hand coming up with his gun. But Glass was ready. He drew and fired, seeming to hesitate an instant before the gun, frozen to aim, sent a slug crashing into Billy Grand, shocking him backward. He took two steps forward, apparently recovering, trying to bring his gun to bear. Then he twisted slowly around, his legs crossed at the knees. His head dipped, and he pitched forward. He struck the ground with his hat sliding off so that it was mashed under his head. His arms looked disjointed. He kicked a couple of times spasmodically, and all movement stopped. The echoes of the gunshot were gone, and the trail of smoke from Glass' pistol. Nobody moved as the cattle came on. A horsefly lit on the back of Grand's neck and crawled leisurely, drinking his sweat.

"What the hell's going on here?" asked Manning, pulling up after a gallop. He saw Grand and understood. Glass retreated, one hand on the bridge of his horse, gun drawn watching Moffitt, Lejune, the others.

"This had been coming on for a while, Al."

"It's your quarrel, not mine. These cattle are my quarrel. What are you trying to do, turn this herd up and down the river? Get this man out of here."

"Tell his pals to get him out," said Dad. "He can be tromped six feet in the ground for all I care."

"Get him out of here!" Manning said to Lejune.

Lejune and Grumbauer lifted him

from the ground. His loose weight was unmanageable; and one of them put a rope around his body, under the armpits, took a dally around the saddle horn, and pulled him away through the grass, through tangled brush to a sage-covered flat.

"They'll wear him out before they can bury him," someone remarked.

"His gun's still down there," said Goings. "Somebody better get his gun. It's worth twenty-five dollars."

"Worth mor'n twenty-five. It's got pearl handles."

Moffitt rode through cattle and picked it up without getting from his horse and when he came up with the pistol in his hand, Glass thought he might try to fire. But several of the emigrant bunch had rifles out, so he merely put it inside an empty saddlebag as he rode away.

"He doesn't seem so upset about his pal," said Dad.

"He's glad to get the free gun," Goings said.

The river was not large but branching and wide. It flowed in several channels with islands between. Earlier in the year, when the snow water was roaring down from the mountains, the grassy meadow itself was an island. Now dry channels with mud-scummed rocks in their bottoms bounded it. The channels were eight or ten feet deep, and turned the cattle. A massed and heaving jam developed in the stream as some cattle tried to come over and others turned back. Cattle bawled and hooked one another and climbed over one another's backs.

"Hi-ya!" the cowboys were shouting. With goads and prod poles they tried to get the cattle broken into groups and moving.

"It's no use," Dad said, finding Glass. "We'll never cut this herd tonight. They're jamming that main bunch right over us."

"Where are those son of a bitching emigrants?" Manning was calling. "Frye, you and your kids get over and manage the swing bunch."

But the swing bunch came down, adding to the jam of cattle. A great many cattle were down and mired, but there was a hard bottom about belly-deep and all but a few struggled to the far side. The sun was at the horizon, and a golden dust drifted over the river. Broadbaker, working the drag like the poorest cowboy, came up dust-coated, his lips and eyes ringed with mud.

"Keep 'em moving! Hi-ya! What's holding you up over there?"

He had been downstream, where his wagon, in crossing had turned over. Everything he owned was soaked, and he'd had trouble finding men to get it on its wheels again. He was tired and angry. He rode up with his legs thrust out in the stirrups. He sat, lean-waisted and heavy-shouldered, with the heels of his hands resting on his thighs. "You, McCoy!" he shouted in a dirt-roughened voice. "What are you doing with those cattle?"

"I'm getting my stock out of the

herd. I'm heading north right here."

"Whose decision is that?"

McCoy didn't answer the question. Some of the cattle had Tilted A Arbogast brands, and some the Rafter 6, also Arbogast.

Broadbaker shouted, "Those are Arbogast cattle! What in hell's got into you?"

He sat stubbornly and said, "It may be they are, but I was told to cut 'em out with ours."

"Who told you?"

"Glass."

"You must have misunderstood him. This whole thing must be a mistake. We're driving this bunch up from the river. We can't leave 'em in the brush and the quicksand."

"I didn't misunderstand anybody."

"Then don't misunderstand me, either. *Hay ya!* Get 'em out of there." He rode back and forth shouting "*Hay ya!* and swinging a knotted rope goad.

McCoy, tired and angry, tried to stand against him, and when the cattle pushed on, mixing with his cut, he called Broadbaker, "a dirty man-eater."

Broadbaker drew up as if he had been spit on. He was carrying a short-barreled rifle squeezed between his waist and the saddle. He grabbed it in one hand and turned the horse with the other. He did it with such power that the horse almost fell. While the horse righted itself McCoy got back a little. One of his sons had a gun, and there was a man of Denison's. Broadbaker swept them with a glance. He wasn't afraid of them, all three, but he wasn't the man to go up against odds not in his favor. Not unless it couldn't be avoided and it almost always could.

"You better look out who you start kicking around in this camp, Broadbaker!" McCoy said, apparently frightened by his temerity but knowing he had the men with him. "Unless you want some of the same that Billy Grand got."

"What about Billy?"

"He got what he's been looking for. He got a bullet through his dirty heart."

"Who from?"

"Glass! Glass outdrew him and killed him!"

Broadbaker's face lay in savage lines. He sat with the rifle staring at McCoy, who went on.

"That son of a bitch Grand! He shot a kid. A thirteen-year-old kid."

"What kid are you talking about?" Broadbaker asked.

"You know who! The Pattison kid."

"McCoy!" said Denison's cowboy. "Keep quiet!"

"No," said Broadbaker, "I want to hear this."

"You heard all I'm going to tell you," McCoy said. He had been shooting scared and now he wanted to get back out of the way.

"McCoy, if I'm supposed to have shot some kid, I want to know about it. You say it's the Pattison kid? Did somebody find a body?"

"They found more'n a body."

"I think they found him alive," Al Manning said.

Where is he?"

"I don't know."

"Who told you that?"

"There's talk around."

"Why do you want to know?" yelled one of the McCoy boys. "So you can go and finish the job?"

"No! Because I want to get at the truth of it. This is my outfit. Do I look like a man who needs to go around blasting kids? If Billy Grand . . . "

But it was no use. He could no longer be heard over the onward surge of the cattle.

20

Gaunt and Savage Giant

BROADBAKER had slept no more than two or three hours the night before. Or the night before that. He could not recall one instance in the last couple of weeks when he had slept through from supper till breakfast. That and the riding and the heat had beaten him down. It gave him the feeling of having been hammered on an anvil. It had sharpened him, giving all his senses a ragged razor edge. He felt as if there were vinegar in his blood. The sun hurt his eyes. Sounds struck hard against eardrums that seemed stretched too tight. But still he could see and hear with unusual acuteness. He could *feel* things. He was at his best, actually. A man rising against adversity.

For the last couple of days he had felt something amiss. He had a sense of impending crisis. He felt like a man riding toward a precipice. The Pattison kid had not troubled him much. In fact, after that bit of business, after saying good night to Grand and Moffitt, he had slept the best he had in many nights. Now, apparently, the kid had survived. He began putting small evidences together. There had been Pedro and Glass with some secret, and an edginess among the emigrants. But what he noticed most was the way Lon Arbogast was acting. As a rule, he drove his wagon slowly, lagging a little to spare the horses, but suddenly he developed the habit of being far over to the north, or urging his team so hard he got out past the cookwagon. It seemed sometimes as if he were tempted to escape entirely. Then, when he rode over to talk to him, Polly would meet him. She always just happened to be there. She would engage him in conversation and urge him to go somewhere with her. Often she made the thinnest kind of excuse and led him to believe she wanted him to care for her in a physical manner. This was not unpleasant, even though he knew she had some motive as yet unexplained.

It never occurred to him that they were hiding the Pattison kid. How could it — he had seen him dead. He had seen the blood and the way he was lying with his head driven into the soft dirt. He had every look of a dead person — there was simply no doubt of it. He could not shoot because of the night riders snooping. Now he wished he had gone down and knocked him in the back of the head or used his jackknife to cut his throat.

But there was no doubt of it. Wounded, the kid was alive. He had been bullet-shocked to simulate death. It could happen being hit by one of those big .45 caliber bullets. Somebody — Pedro, no doubt — had found him. Pedro and Glass. Then, watching their time, Lon Arbogast drove around and got him in the wagon. Polly was in on it. They had hauled him for two days in their wagon, hiding him. From him, Broadbaker. From him, the man who had got them loose from their debts, saved a herd for them. Their lack of gratitude cut him. He felt a violent reaction to injustice. He had given all he could to them, done it from the generosity of his being, given his heart blood and had been paid back in gall. He wanted Polly to become his wife, but there had been no condition stated. He had merely *given* and had trusted her in return. And now this. This! He laughed through his teeth as he rode, and the laugh became a sob and a curse. He wanted to strike out against her and against all the world. He had done everything for them. For the emigrants, too. Against their own stubbornness, poverty, and stupidity he had tried to make them share his goal and a shining future, to drop them into the greatest ranching land in all the west. And in payment they hated him, connived behind his back, and even grew so bold as to stand up and defy him to his face. Like McCoy, that cur, that yapping dog.

He rode the high ground, where the light lingered. He had a view of the river and the rising country. His men were following orders, driving the cattle on. As long as they were driven hard, nobody could cut the herd. It was impossible for Ted Goings to get out his twenty-seven, or Brown his dozen, and certainly no chance for all the beef controlled by Glass, or the four hundred-odd head owned by Frye.

Far away he could see the top of the cookwagon with a point of red from the flag. Braskin had some wood in a bundle and was dragging it along the ground kicking up a trail of dust that looked pinkish in the sunset. At last he saw what he was looking for. Far over to the north, just rolling around the brow of a hill, was Lon Arbogast's homewagon. He was obviously trying to get out of sight. If Broadbaker had not ridden to the high country, he might never have seen him.

"The son of a bitch," he said bitterly. "The weak, ungrateful son of a bitch!"

He rode back across the trampled ground and forded the river. The cattle had long been over, all of them, and the water was clearing. His horse stepped in a deep part and swam for a while. The water, rolling over Broadbaker's legs and filling his boots, felt good and cold. The boys were still driving, and some of them had made torches of dry, shredded aspen bark to come down on the drag and scorch them into running. "*Hi-ya! Hi-ya!*" the men shouted, as they always did. Once in a while one would have a special cry, such as "*Zup-a-ya!*" which was the Lambert fellow they called 'Rolla' after his town in Missouri, or Ed Dixon, who kept saying "*hup-hup-hup!*"

"How about it?" Al Manning asked, coming over on a fresh horse, at least his eighth for that hard, long day.

"How far do you want this to go on? They're getting a little ringy."

"They're not going to run — you can see that."

"No, they won't run now, but let 'em bed down for an hour and then see. It's always that way when they get too strung-out tired. They settle in, and then some little thing startles them. All of a sudden you have four thousand cattle jumping right out of their hides to hit the ground a-running."

"When they run, Al, just see to it they run toward the Popo Agie."

"Did you hear about Grand?"

"I heard about him."

"I have an idea that Moffitt, Lejune, and those fellows will be gunning for Glass and not too particular whether they get him from in front or behind."

"That's Glass' worry. He must have known what he was doing when he tossed down on Billy."

"Well, all right. But Glass has his bunch, too. I wouldn't want any full-scale battles."

"And you won't get any. It sounds like a standoff. I don't know any better way to keep the peace, absolutely and forever, than by a standoff."

Dark came rapidly. Some cloud banks had been moving around, quenching the sunset. The north and west were the color of bullet lead, and one could feel the disquiet of distant lightning. It was very still, but here and there an air current came and stirred the grass. It seemed unusually warm. Broadbaker noticed how the coat of his horse was filled with electricity. He could pass his hand over the animal's coat, not touching, and the hair would crackle and stand. Not all of it, but here and there a bit, so that the sheen was disturbed. There hadn't been a single person struck by lightning or a horse or a wagon since the start. Tonight might be the night. He got to thinking it might be him and that in a single flash all he had fought for could be wiped out. Peculiarly it wasn't dying he worried about but the loss of his property and being cut off midway in the trail. And those filthy, squawking emigrants tramping over his grave. And Polly with Glass! She was always by accident where Glass happened to be. He had even considered stopping the herd and letting Glass cut out for Montana, letting all of them cut out for Montana but he needed them to win the Popo Agie. After they were all on the Popo, with winter coming and no way to leave, he'd know how to take care of the whole situation. Then he'd have the answer for all who thought they could spit in his face!

He rode to the top of the knoll around which Lonnie's homewagon had disappeared, expecting to see it farther along, just a little way, but there was nothing but the empty sag of a wash. Bulberries and a sort of rabbit brush grew here and there in the bottom, which was a series of steplike saucers, washouts of white dirt. He rode down and across through the grabbing wires of the brush. It was too dark to see the twigs that reached out and ripped his skin, drawing beads of blood. He did not mind pain, it kept him alert, he rather enjoyed it, it fed his anger, the vinegar in his veins. Wagon wheels were deeply printed in the soft ground. It seemed to be a low divide but was actually a turn and a shoulder of the dry wash. Then he saw the wagon.

It had stopped. It was standing with its hindside toward him. Someone had come over with a fresh team. The team was being hitched, and the old ones being driven away by one of the horse wranglers. Apparently Lon was not stopping for the night. A fresh team meant he had lots of travel yet on his mind. It meant he must be heading for Montana right here and expecting his herd to follow.

Lon, stepping away from the wagon, called quietly to the wrangler through cupped hands, "Hey! If you see Leo Glass over there, tell him to come around, will you?"

"Yah, Mr. Arbogast."

Neither of them saw Broadbaker. Senses alert, he rode on slowly. His horse made hardly a sound on the soft earth. There were some closer flicks of lightning. He could feel the thunder across his back. The wind, after circling with a humming sound through the sage, dipped into the draw and rippled his shirt, cooling him under the armpits. It flapped the canvas of the wagon, and getting inside, filled it like a balloon. Lon Arbogast went hurrying around, tightening it. The balloon of the canvas was so strong at times that it lifted the wagon, which was joggling on its springs. Someone was talking inside, and Lonnie answering him.

"You lie down," he was saying. "It looks like a blow with some rain in it."

"Hello, Lonnie," Broadbaker said, not loud.

Lon Arbogast spun and faced him. He had a caught look of a man hiding guilt. He had the sick, drained look of a man afraid to die.

21

End of a Partnership

"WHAT'S the trouble, Lon?" asked Broadbaker in the most pleasant voice he could manage. "Aren't you glad to see me? I've always been a good friend of yours, Lon. I've proved it, Lon. Don't we confide anymore? If something's the trouble, why not tell me?"

"Nothing is the trouble!"

"Why are you stopping away over here?"

"Goddammit, because — " Whatever he started to say, he changed his mind. "There's storm coming up. I want to be away from those cattle. And ready to roll. That's why the fresh team."

"It's no safer here than anyplace."

"I used the lower crossing. I had to travel and travel to find a place. I came up here, and it was dark. It seems like as good a place as any."

"There's been something troubling you, Lon," he said, getting down.

"I told you nothing was the trouble."

Broadbaker genuinely could not understand it. He had done everything for this man. He had always used him with the utmost consideration. Even when he made a decision, one that had to be, he always went around and talked to Lon, pretending he had to be consulted. That kid inside couldn't be the real reason. It was upsetting to find him shot, but one kid more or less was simply not that important to an Arbogast. He was just another dirt-floor cabin kid, the kind that came rolling west, gangling and shaggy, shoeless, with one suspender, a tow-sacking shirt, freckled, snaggle-toothed, and with the shakes. You could send your hounds through the bottoms back in Missouri and drive them out like the hogs. You saw them by the dozens and the hundreds rolling west, loud and ignorant. The wagon families had such kids in litters like hound dogs, filling the camp grounds, filling the work gangs, filling the graves. Lon Arbogast, of all people, had to have a proper contempt for such back-country riffraff. It was too bad about what had happened but it ought to be perfectly obvious that it couldn't be helped. After all, what was one wagon whelp more or less when compared with the success of outfits such as Broadbaker's or Arbogast's? You didn't see the railroad worrying about killing a few Irishmen or Chinamen, did you? He just couldn't understand why Lon was making such a thing of it. So it had to be something else.

"You got that kid in there, haven't you?"

"Stay away from him!"

"Don't give me orders, Lonnie. You know the agreement we made when we started out. You were anxious enough to give me full authority then."

"What do you intend to do?"

"Good God, what can I do? It was a mistake to bring him back here, sure. But Grand did it. And he died for it. That's been quite a sacrifice on our part. I let that son of a bitch Glass kill him and didn't lift a hand. But now we have to take this kid out and get rid of him. You know the trouble we're likely to have otherwise. The army and all. You know how they're going to take this kid's story, if we let him go off yapping, and stretch it and enlarge it and make it out a whole damned conspiracy like they did down in Nebraska. Don't think this is the sort of a task I enjoy. It isn't. But there are a lot of unpleasant jobs to do, the thing is to *do* it. Do it as quick as you can and then forget about it. It's the way your grandfather did when he came west and tore his domain from the hands of the Sioux and the Pawnee. Believe me, this looks important now, but once this kid is out of the way and out of his misery and under the dirt and the cattle driven over him, it'll seem like he never was."

"Andy, what kind of an animal are you? A wolf off the prairie wouldn't — "

"You're calling me that, Lonnie? You calling me a wolf off the prairie after all I've done for you?"

Lonnie retreated around the wagon with Broadbaker following him. He might have run, but he shot a glance at the wagon, showing he did not dare leave with the wounded boy inside. Backing, he failed to notice a clump of sage and fell over it. He managed to drop on one side, and his right hip was free. In that position he went for his gun, but Broadbaker sprang and booted it from his hands. Lonnie dived for the gun and got hold of it, and Broadbaker, waiting half a second, jumped and came down on his forearm with both feet. He had his arm under the high insteps of his boots, pinning it to the ground. And he turned, grinding, bearing down with all his weight.

He felt the bones crack. It was a good feeling. He liked Lonnie's scream of pain. It did him more good than a fine cigar or a drink of whiskey. It gratified him deep down. He was giving Lon Arbogast what he deserved. It was not just a recent feeling that this man had failed him. Broadbaker admired authority. He had never himself with willingness undermined those established in wealth and power. He had felt himself one of them. But when they failed, he felt that he was being diminished with them. With the Arbogasts he had made every effort not to see their degradation. He had tried to make it cease to be by bolstering them. He had even intended to take Polly as his wife. He had had a wife and several children in Texas, but that was before the war, and now he had every reason to believe that she was dead. His inquiries to a lawyer in San Antonio had failed to locate them. So he considered that part of his life washed out, settled, to be closed and forgotten, and he intended to take Polly as his wife and give her the honor, the greatest honor any man can pay a woman, of having her bear his sons. The sons who would inherit his name and all he had worked for. These thoughts were all with him as he twisted back and forth, splintering and grinding the bones. Lon had rolled around in a half-circle, held by the arm, and in pain he had filled his mouth with dirt. Now he was on his back with teeth peeled back and eyes staring, and his voice was an inhaling, thin scream of pain.

He had had enough for the time being. Broadbaker picked up the pistol and stepped back. He did not know yet whether to kill him. It was something that required thought. After killing him, there was no way of undoing it. Lonnie deserved to die, he was a quitter, he was trying to cut out and go to Montana, but Broadbaker still needed the Arbogasts, their influence. Would Lon now cooperate? If so, could he be trusted? If he killed him and the kid both, would word of it get out? How would he conceal the bodies? Never again would he make the mistake of having men killed and burned inside their cabins. Even the ranchers, the eastern interests, the Englishmen, and the other powerful and great who were feeling the land-grabber's pressure, the ones he was fighting for as much as for himself, had turned against him that time.

Moaning, Lon Arbogast staggered to his feet. He used his left hand to lift his right. He stood holding the splintered bones together.

"I didn't want to do that, Lon, but you made me." He could not comprehend what he was saying. "Lon, I'll get your arm patched up, and it'll be all right. Just promise me there won't be any more trouble."

Lon backed around the wagon. It was dark enough so that he could almost escape by diving beneath, darting one way or the other or coming up behind the horses, which he could get to running and, with Broadbaker momentarily afoot, escape. Or there might be a gun inside.

"I don't want to hurt you, Lon. I really don't. Why, you mean a lot to me, Lon. We've just had a misunderstanding."

Lon did not seem to understand a word. He kept staring at the gun in Broadbaker's hand. He bent forward, still holding the dangling, useless arm, and pretended to stumble. Then he dived under the wagon.

Broadbaker had to get some distance. He sprang back and in that position could see Lon's progress beneath. There was no place for him to go except beyond the front wheels. He was hidden, and Broadbaker had to make up his mind. There was only one thing he could do. There was no chance of Lon's cooperating, so he had to kill him. First him and then the kid. Then he would drive off with their bodies in the wagon. He would hide everything somehow.

The storm was providential. At last it seemed that God was favoring him. His run of bad luck would have to change. With long, panther-light steps he circled the rear. He could see Lon Arbogast's legs. He had the pistol poised. But a gun roared from inside the wagon. The kid! He happened to be moving, and the bullet missed. He felt the lash and smell of the powder, the burn of it. He fell flat, expecting the second charge of a double gun. The second shot did not come, and he realized that it was the old single-shot deer rifle always kept in the wagon. It was a cap-and-ball piece and would take time to reload.

He came to one knee and tried to see Lon among the horses' legs. One of the horses wanted to run, and the other delayed. Wind was whipping the sage, and the wagon seemed to be jumping on its springs. He thought he saw a man crawling, so he fired. On the wind a girl's voice came to him, and the thudding of hoofs. Was it Polly — or his imagination? Wind and dark and lightning played tricks with his hearing and his sight. He fired twice more. The team was running now. The wagon lurched behind them. They turned, crashed into the brush and through it, and up the far bench. He looked for Lon on the ground. He ran after the wagon. Dust was pouring behind it. He saw Lon holding to the back, being dragged. Somehow he had got the endgate with his good arm, and his boots dragged the dirt. Broadbaker cursed and fired both guns empty aiming at man, wagon top, even the horses pulling it.

Then he was alone. He had been vaguely aware of someone galloping by. That was Polly. How much had she seen? But what difference? All now would be out in the open as it should be, as it should have been all the time.

He caught his horse. Gaunt and savage, he mounted, and when the horse proved fractious, he spurred blood from its sides. He laughed into the wind and said, "You dirty bitches. You ungrateful, back-biting sons of bitches!"

He was through apologizing before the world. He was finished with standing hat in hand. With the Arbogasts, with everybody. He had tried the soft approach and now he would go forth like an honest man and take what he had paid for. He would find Polly and have her. He would rip the clothes off her and mount her on the ground. It was what she really wanted. It was what women always wanted, screams and importuning to the contrary. They wanted to be had by the strongest. They wanted to be impregnated by a real, honest-to-God man. He would kill anyone who got in his way. The wild, flashing night was part of his mood.

Then he turned and saw Polly riding up the dry wash directly toward him.

22

Tidal Wave of Beef

AT last Frogs Braskin stopped his cookwagon to make camp. There was an early darkness, and a storm was coming up. It was not the usual dry rain of a Wyoming evening, one that came black with distant mutterings and cleared away to show the stars from one horizon to the other by ten o'clock. This one promised to be a real gully washer, with lightnings from rim to rim and wind in black torrents. Everyone was particularly hungry, having put in a longer than usual day on shorter than usual rations, but Braskin was having his trouble with the fire. It burned and scattered coals on the wind, once getting the wagon top a blaze, but even with the help of some big sheet-metal reflector plates it refused to deliver its heat to the stewpot.

Glass rode past the wagon and saw that nothing but a miracle passing of the storm would yield supper before midnight. The herd was up and milling around. When the lightning flashed, he could see the shine of tossing horns. He wondered where Lon Arbogast's wagon was. He saw the other Arbogast wagons but not Lon's. Then he caught sight of Polly.

"Polly!" he called, but the wind and the bawling sucked up his voice.

He rode, looking for her. He stopped with a view of the river and turned back. The storm kept coming closer. It seemed to charge the entire atmosphere — the grass, the surface of the earth, and all things on it. Everything was magnetized. In the dense clarity before the storm one could see the backs of cattle with an electric glow like an aurora. No sign of Polly. There were some small coulees to the north. It was the only place she could have gone. The homewagon would be there. Of course Lon would cross the river lower down and come up in their concealment. He decided to get a new horse. The remuda was at hand, and he rode up, motioning for the wrangler to bring over another of the Y2 string, a sand-colored roan. While stripping his saddle off he heard a gunshot.

The wrangler, already nervous at being around horses with all the lightning, said, "Who in hell did that? Al Manning will have somebody's hide if he starts these cattle to running."

"After the way he's been flogging them all day? I don't think they have much run left."

"They're all up and trembling. They get to moving around in small bunches, and it's a bad sign. When they get to wall-eyed bawling after dark and climbing over each other, watch out! Any little sound is likely to start 'em. In fact, the little sounds are more likely to start them than the big ones."

Then he heard other shots, as many

as eight or nine. They seemed to be coming from the coulees. He mounted and rode away. He was on a long legged horse that was a good traveler and a hard runner but not easy to turn and perhaps for that reason a poor choice on such a night. Anyhow he hadn't been saddled in a couple of days and hence was willing to go.

Suddenly a wagon rolled into view. It was a runaway. He heard Polly and thought she was driving. He spurred in that direction. There was nobody in the wagon seat, but someone was hanging to the rear. He had the endgate under one armpit, and his boots were dragging behind, stirring the dust. By flashes of lightning he saw Lon Arbogast's face. It might have been the set, cold face of a dead man.

He spurred to a gallop and reached the team. He was able to guide them in one direction but not the other. Suddenly the cookwagon loomed ahead. Braskin ran out waving a gunnysack. The team swerved to one side. Somewhere back in the dark Lon Arbogast had fallen off. Cattle were all around. The herd was running. It was a stampede, but they were running on both sides at nearly the speed of the horses. It was like being in a boat, carried by a mighty current. He had the feeling that he could at any time get up and walk across their backs.

He heard young Will shouting from inside the wagon.

"Will?"

"Yah! Who is it? Glass?"

"Hold tight!"

"What's goin' on out there? What's goin' on?" he kept yelling, but Glass was too busy to answer.

The cattle pressed close, threatening to crush the wagon. Then they seemed to split into two rivers of movement, and the wagon was on open ground. He was just getting the team under control when there was a sudden steep drop, and the wagon pitched forward with a splintered axle. The horses went down with the wagon half over them

239

and came up fighting the harness. Dismounting, he managed to cut them free of the tugs and hold them by the bridles.

It had started to rain. The rain came in great, dust-filled drops. It drummed, and the hoofs of cattle drummed. Lightning struck close with a singeing flash and a crack like exploding powder. It left a strange, chemical smell. Then the skies opened, and the rain was a torrent. It closed in all around. It seemed even to shut out the lightning and thunder. The rain was a peace after chaos, soaking him, making his clothes stick to his body, weighting his hat, flowing a stream from the front gutter of the brim as he freed the horses and got them around to the leeward side and tied their heads close in against the wagon. Through rips of lightning, like rents in the storm, he could see out across a splashing sea.

"Leo?" the kid was calling. "Leo, are you out there?"

He did not want to shout back before

getting the team secure.

"Leo! Leo!" the kid kept calling.

"Here I am," he said, getting through the endgate door.

"Oh, are you all right?"

"Am I all right? Are you all right? You're the wounded one."

"Well, I got jolted around a little. A lot of stuff came loose. What happened?"

"The cattle ran — we outran 'em. Then we went down over a little bank and smashed the front ax."

His matches were all wet. One side of him was as wet as if he had fallen in the river, and that, of course, was where the matches were.

"Leo?"

"I'm right here." He groped and touched a foot. The kid seemed to have rolled to the low corner. He was half sitting, with his legs out.

"You've sure had it rough, kid."

"Where's Lonnie?"

"He's all right." He didn't know he was all right, but falling off where he must have, there was little danger from the cattle.

"Broadbaker didn't kill him, then?"

"I didn't see anything of Broadbaker. Was that him shooting?"

"Mostly. But I got a shot at *him*." He snuffled and used some men's words, blaming himself for having a chance at close range and missing.

"That's all right. You're too young to start carving notches in a gun."

"I tried to get up front and drive. I just couldn't make it — what with all the jouncing around."

"You did real well, Will. I'm proud of you. Don't they keep any matches around?"

"Yonder, in the lift-front case."

There was a prolonged lightning flash, which made the inside almost as light as day. He could see clothes and blankets tumbled around, the kid sitting with his eyes big, and a latch-front cabinet. He found the matches in a tin can. He lit one, but a draft blew it out. He lit another and found a candle. The candle holder had a small chimney that had rolled around without breaking. He found a place to hang it. Rain poured through holes and seams, and he could see the white inside scars where the bullets had torn through the wagon box.

"Won't that light draw 'lectricity?" ask Will.

"No, we're pretty safe here. The river is drawing it."

He fixed the kid's bed and got him around with his head uphill. Then he had a look at the bandage. It had hardened, but the dampness was soaking it up.

"You've sure gone to a lot of bother with me."

"You'd have been better off if you'd never met me."

"Did you know they cut up my new hat? They — "

"Well, they won't do it any more. Grand won't."

"Did you kill him, Leo?"

"Yes."

"I knew you would! I was telling Mr. Arbogast you would. I said, just you wait — "

"Don't talk any more now. You seem to be getting along all right. The jouncing didn't make the wound open."

"I feel 'most good enough to get up."

"You lie here and sleep. It's black as a gambler's heart outside or will be when the lightning passes, and nobody will find you. You're as safe as you'd be in camp. Safer. I'm going to leave for a while. Here, I'll leave my gun."

"You'll need it."

"I won't need it. Anyway, I'll come back in an hour or so and get it."

"I got the rifle, if you'll load it for me. I can't work the ramrod all stove up — "

"You take the pistol, kid. I know where I can get another."

"Well, okay."

"But don't just cut loose at some sound. Lie right still. If anybody calls, don't answer unless you know who it is. Keep quiet and keep the gun." He was telling him too much. The thing for him to get was some rest. The gun would give him confidence. "You don't mind?"

"No, I'll be all right, boss."

23

Search in the Darkness

THE rain and the lightning had diminished. A cold wind sprang up, carrying the fine spray-end of storm. Glass rode one of the draft horses bareback, using a rope and halter.

The herd had left trampled mud, but he found better going in the sod of the prairie. In the distance, men were shouting. It was very dark, there was not a star, and the lightning was distant. It had moved far to the south, beyond stacks of clouds. Water ran in heavy streams down every gully. Ahead of him lay the valley of the North Fork, a dark depression in the dark country.

"Hey, there!" a man said, riding almost into him. "Is that you, Eddie?" It was Tom McCoy.

"No, Glass."

"Glass! I thought you were dead. I saw your horse going like blazes with the saddle empty."

"No, I got on the Arbogast wagon. The kid was in it."

"Pattison?"

"Yes."

"How is he?"

"So far he's in good shape. I don't think the bullet got inside. It seemed to crack some ribs and make him bleed. I think he's going to be all right."

"Then *you* were driving the wagon that started this mess!"

"You can say it if you want to, but Broadbaker started it when he cut loose at Lon Arbogast."

"He shot at Arbogast? God help the poor prairie dogs when the wolves get to fighting."

"You haven't heard anything of Lon?"

"No."

"Or Broadbaker?"

"Him, either. Manning's over there

yelling so you can hear him a mile, trying to get the cattle off the river. But how in hell you going to get anything done this kind of night, and the storm on its way back? I'm hunting for my folks. A couple of wagons were smashed — the herd went right over them. Ours was all right except for the one Herbie was driving, and I can't find it."

"You've seen nothing of Polly?"

"No." Then he called, "Leo! Look out for Moffitt and that bunch."

"Where are they?"

"I heard 'em talking down by that big grove. They're out for you."

"What'd you hear?"

"Nothing much. I just recognized their voices, like a man will in the dark. And they said something about you."

"All right, Tom. Thanks."

The rain stopped, and the clouds began to lift, leaving some stars in view. He rode down on the North Fork. Manning's voice came to him. He was issuing commands and cursing when the men did not carry them out.

"I can't see a thing in here," someone said. "What use is it combing this brush when we'll have to do it again tomorrow?" But he wasn't saying it loud enough for Manning to hear. "I'm soaked. Every time you touch that brush, you get a drenching."

"It's a good thing, Chino," a man said, laughing. "You been needing your yearly bath."

Chino was Chino Stallcop, one of the Arbogast riders. The other voice belonged to a short fellow with a crippled foot, Bob Miller.

He rode past and by accident jumped a couple of cows, which he drove ahead, and Manning, coming that way, mistook him for Chino.

"You made quite a gather!" Manning said. "Is two all you found?"

"Hello, Al."

"Oh, it's you. I thought they'd killed you under the wagon."

"No, I die hard."

Manning, a large, limber man with

a jutting head looked at him through the darkness.

"Well, you started this run, so get busy and help gather."

"I started nothing!"

"I saw that wagon come barreling over the hill and I saw you in the seat. So don't tell me — "

"I am telling you!" He was as tired and hairtriggered as Manning. "That son of a bitch Broadbaker set it off. He was down there to kill the Pattison kid. And Lon." When Manning started to say something, he shouted into his face. "No, you listen for a while! I'm telling you and I'm telling everybody. It was him and Grand and Moffitt that tried to kill the kid. Only, the kid crawled off, and the Arbogasts picked him up. Lon hid him in the wagon. Then Broadbaker heard he was alive and came around to finish it. Go up and look. You'll see bullet holes all through that wagon. I still don't know where Lon is. He was hanging on behind and got pulled off. Maybe he's dead. So don't bellow your head off at me about the stampede. It was your boss the man-eater that started it. You must be proud of working for such a son of a bitch."

"Don't yell at me. I'm just the herd boss. Yell it at him."

"Yah, Glass," said a cowboy named Seltzer, "why don't you ride out and tell him? We'd enjoy hearing it. And burying you afterward."

He despised Seltzer, a great talker of gunfight, and errand man for the Grand bunch.

"Where is he?"

"I saw him down yonder."

Manning glared at Seltzer much as to say *keep your mouth shut*. They were attracting a crowd. Cowboys kept groping up through the brush, soaked and weary.

"Come on!" said Manning. "No more of this. We'll have a hundred cattle mired in the river before morning. Let's chase 'em out of here."

Glass rode north, down the river.

The clouds were breaking, revealing a deep, washed sky. The sky seemed very dark, and the stars larger from the rain. He could see the position of the moon. It was some time coming out, but its light was there in silver reflections around the clouds. It had been so dark for so long that the moon, when it appeared, made it seem almost like day. Very distant now was the sound of thunder. It was almost nothing. An uneasiness along the horizon. The water had all run away. Now and then some movement caused a slight patter of droplets caught on the leaves. With the cattle behind, it was exquisitely still.

Some men had made a fireless camp nearby. He could smell tobacco smoke. They fell silent, watching his approach. A voice and a laugh — Lejune. Grumbauer said something. They would kill him on sight, but he had not been recognized. Bareback on the workhorse, he was taken for one of the emigrants.

"Hey, hoe-man!" said Grumbauer.

"He ain't speaking tonight."

"Hey, hoe-man — you looking for your cows?"

"Yah, it's milkin' time."

"He's looking for his old lady."

"We got her here in the bushes, hoe-man."

"Hoe-man, lost your tongue?"

"Listen, I'm talking to you!" Grumbauer said, walking out. He stopped suddenly when he recognized Glass. He said not a word.

"Who is it?" asked Moffitt.

"Why, hello, *Glass*," Grumbauer said in mock cordiality.

He stopped, not wanting to show himself in the moon. Then he was relieved to hear Dad's voice.

"It's all right, Leo. I got 'em covered."

A man fired. The bullet flicked past, cutting the twigs. A gun — Dad's — answered. Both were unexpectedly close, and he could smell the trail of burnt powder. His horse nearly ran from under him. He could hear someone cursing and panting in the brush. It sounded like Moffitt.

Other guns cut loose and as instantly ended. There were seven or eight shots, one tight on the other, and then silence.

He managed to slow his horse. Galloping over those bottoms was more dangerous than blind gunfire. Then he heard a girl's voice at some distance. It was Polly, it could be no one but Polly, and she seemed to be calling his name.

24

What Happened to Polly

WHEN Polly Arbogast rode over the little hill in the lightning-laced blackness before storm, she did not at first notice the wagon. Its white top, seen from above, matched closely the whiteness of some alkali patches in the step-like bottom of the draw. She knew that Lon had crossed the North Fork a mile or two downstream, trying to avoid a meeting with Broadbaker, and hence she believed him still a considerable distance. The proximity of the storm, whose gale winds caught her on the high ground, gave her added reason to hurry, and she might have passed the wagon without seeing it at all except for the gunshot. It was the single-shot rifle. She recognized it. The gun, with its long barrel and heavy steel, gave a sharp, small, high-intensity sound that always echoed in a certain manner. She looked then and saw the wagon.

She called, but distance and the wind intervened. She rode at a stiff trot, watching. There was a saddle horse nearby, and men were in view. Then, during a long brightness, when twin currents of lightning laced across the sky, she saw it all frozen like a camera exposure — her brother apparently hurt and trying to get away around the front of the outfit, Broadbaker with a pistol in each hand.

She screamed — spontaneously, suddenly, with a sudden impact of sound that caused Broadbaker to move, and she knew by the flash and her brother's diving lunge that the bullet had missed.

Her horse, turning because of the cry and the gunshot, almost unseated her. She grabbed and held tight. The team was running. She could see the wagon careening, and behind them the lacing of gunfire and more shots than she could count.

She called, "Lon! Lon!" and got no answer. Someone rode down, galloping, got beside the wagon, and climbed to the seat. It was Glass. She knew his manner, the long swing of his body silhouetted by flashes of light. Then she was caught in the rip and grasp of brush at the bottom of the draw and when she got out, Broadbaker was there.

She wanted to follow the wagon, but it would be necessary to get around him. She tried to do so by riding across the wash, but her horse was tired. He slipped in making a short climb. He was half down in crumbly dirt, unable to get up. She got out of the saddle, and still he had trouble pawing to his four feet. He backed around, and she held him by the bridle. Broadbaker reined in and watched her.

"Polly!" he said.

"Where's Lon?"

"Lon's all right. Here, can I help you?"

She let him take hold of the bridle. She was frightened of him. For the first time she felt an actual fright and a desire to escape. She did not ask him about the shooting. There seemed to be a momentary safety in pretended ignorance. A chance to get back to the camp, to the others . . .

"They shot at me first, Polly," he said.

He was breathing hard from an end of effort and excitement. He seemed to want to collect all his faculties before going on. In the meantime he kept hold of her bridle. There came a noise of shouting and a thunder of hoofs from over the hill. It took a second for him to recover and take notice. Then he cursed and said," Good God, they're up and running. The cattle. It's a stampede!"

The herd topped the hill and came directly toward them. She found herself riding and at a gallop, her bridle still in Broadbaker's grasp. There were cattle all around them. Then her horse fell.

She had no recollection of the fall, only that she was alone, walking. The cattle were gone. It was quiet and raining. She walked and walked. Finally Pedro saw her and gave her a boost behind his saddle. There was mud all over her. The cantle felt gritty when she touched it.

She asked how long since the cattle had passed. Pedro was uncertain of time, but he guessed at an hour.

She was still stunned from her fall or from the effects of fatigue and excitement. She could not remember getting to the river and the sound of cattle, but she was there, and someone was assisting her to the ground.

"A stirrup, miss, a stirrup!" Pedro had dismounted and was holding a stirrup to the toe of her boot.

"Catch her!" someone said.

"I'm all right."

She heard Broadbaker ask, "Where did you find her?"

"Walking. She was just out there alone, walking."

"She fell, and her horse got loose. I turned back and hunted for her, but thank God she's all right. Here's something for you." He gave Pedro a five-dollar gold piece. "Polly, listen, Polly," he kept saying. "Polly, are you all right?"

"Yes."

He called for a horse and sent for her saddle. "You're soaked. Aren't you cold?"

"Where's the wagon?"

"I don't know. We haven't located half the wagons. Some were smashed and some made a run for it, and I suppose they're miles off in this darkness. Anyhow we can get out of the damp brush. It's like a cold bucket every time you touch it."

She rode with him down the river. There was starlight now and a hint of the moon. He met someone and talked. She heard a voice she thought was Moffitt's. She heard Glass' name spoken. Only that, just the name. Then it came to her, as if out of dreaming, that they were planning to kill him.

"No!" she said.

"What's the trouble?" he asked.

"What did you tell him?"

"Who?"

"Moffitt?"

"Nothing. Just some instructions."

She thought of her brother, also. He had murdered Lon. "Lon!" she called.

"What's the matter with you? You've been dreaming."

"You killed him!"

He took hold of the bridle, and she ripped it away from him. She struck out blindly at his face. "Let me go!"

"Polly! I'm not taking any more of this, Polly."

"You killed Lon, just like you tried to kill that boy!"

"Yes, your turncoat brother! He turned against me. A no-good, a wastrel. Going through your family fortune. Racehorses, wine, carriages. He has no strength. No backbone. Polly! Listen to me! Just sit and listen!

I didn't kill him. I should have. He's no good. He has no strength. You have strength, Polly. You have the strength of the Arbogasts. You, Polly. You know it, and I know it. Let's be honest. *We* have strength. You're a good deal like me. We're what hold this outfit together. Why lie any longer?"

He came close to her, and she feared his strength. She sensed that things had changed. The truth had finally come out. All the truth. He was not going to lie about young Pattison. About his lust for her. About his wife in Texas, his man-burning, nothing. Their knees were together. She could feel the warmth of his breath and his body. She leaned away and sensed the futility of striking again with the reins. She knew it was useless trying to escape him.

"Polly, I want you. I've wanted you from the start. You were the reason I bailed out the Arbogasts. Because I wanted *you*. From the first moment I wanted to have kids by you."

He could have broken her arm. He

could have crushed her, it seemed, by simply closing his one hand. But she sobbed and twisted, trying to get away.

"Goddammit, it's no little thing I'm offering you. A man tells a woman he wants her to have his sons. The ones who will live after him and carry on all he's worked for. And I'm going to have it, Polly. I'm going to have you."

"How about your family in Texas?" she cried.

"What of the family in Texas? I haven't heard of them in years. There is no worry about that. I went to law. This is a long way from Texas. A long way. I've made a new life. And I've waited a long time. Court records and preachers be damned. Polly . . . "

She fought him, and there was a sound of distant gunfire. Broadbaker paused to listen, and she heard the tone of a voice familiar and welcome. It belonged to Glass. She cried out and she heard it again. She called his name, and with a curse Broadbaker struck her.

"You bitch!" he said through his teeth. "You little ungrateful bitch. You'd choose him, that long rider. You've been chasing off to meet him in the bushes, haven't you? Haven't you?" He held her by the wrist and struck her back-handed across the face, and a numbness spread, so she could no longer feel the blows. She turned from side to side trying to escape, and droplets of blood flew — she could see the dark spatter in the moonlight. "This my pay, you bitch! My reward for rescuing your family. This, this!"

She kept screaming without knowing it, so Glass was almost on them before either realized.

"Polly!"

"Yes!"

Broadbaker let her go then and turned, drawing his pistol. She seized his arm, and while attempting to wrench free he pulled her off the saddle. He tried to fling her away, but she hung.

"Leo! Leo!" she kept saying.

He kicked her in the belly getting free. Glass was there, dismounted, running. Broadbaker aimed point blank at his chest and pulled the trigger. The hammer fell on a discharged chamber. He cocked and pulled three times more, each time with a dead click. All of the chambers were empty. He had never reloaded after firing on the wagon.

But Glass came empty-handed. Broadbaker rammed the gun in its holster and faced him. He let his hands fall to his waist as though in hitching up his trousers, but he unbuckled his gunbelt and, when Glass was close enough, swung the heavy holster like a slingshot. He brought it up and over with all the power of his body, and had it connected at full arc, it would have put his adversary to the ground with a broken neck or at least senseless. However, Glass saw the move at the final instant. He was unable to fall out of range, but he came on, diving under it, and the gun struck him a smashing rib-jarring blow. Part of its force was broken by his arm and shoulder. The gun jammed free, but Broadbaker still had the belt, studded with cartridges. He drove a knee to Leo Glass' groin to get back for another blow. Glass, however, sidestepped and unbuckled his own gunbelt to face him.

Broadbaker laughed. He seemed to take a bitter satisfaction in how things had gone. "All right, I'll fight you Spanish-quirt style."

Glass had once seen two Mexican cowboys duel in that vicious fashion, stripping each other's flesh from bone.

Broadbaker stood with the gunbelt swinging heavy in his right hand, his left extended. He grinned and said, "Well, Glass? What's wrong. Haven't you got the guts for it?"

Men were riding up through the dark. They drew up and were watching. Glass saw from the tail of his eye that some were Broadbaker men, some Arbogast, and some from the emigrant wagons. He extended his hand and said, "I'm ready!"

25

The Duel

THEY locked fingers of their left hands. Glass knew only then how strong Broadbaker was. His fingers were heavy and muscled like a blacksmith's. Once they closed, Glass could not have escaped had he wanted to. They moved, jostling for balance, testing each other's weight and strength, and feeling the damp ground for footing. Broadbaker proved to have a heavy-shouldered advantage in power, but Glass was quicker, and each time Broadbaker came up to feint a blow, Glass moved, making the weight carry him off balance. Then, suddenly, instead of moving forward, Broadbaker stopped with set boots, doubled his left arm, and brought Glass toward him. He swung the gunbelt short, ripping it between them. He attempted to tear out the eyeballs of his adversary with the cartridge-studded loops.

The raking blow rolled Glass' head. He felt it down his spine and across his shoulders. It semed that one side of his face had been torn away. Broadbaker let the force of the blow carry him on. He snapped Glass in a half-pivot. Timing himself he swung a full blow to the unprotected back of Glass' head.

With almost all the loops of the cartridge belt filled, he had in his hand more than a pound of lead. The full swing under his massive power made it a death blow. Too late Glass recognized the maneuver. He could not stop himself from being pivoted, but he let his knees buckle. The weighted belt grazed the back of his head, and he took most of it on his back and right shoulder. He struck the ground sitting, with his feet out. Broadbaker was ready for a still-more-massive swing of the belt. But Glass rolled over, twisting his arm. With a curse of pain Broadbaker was forced to roll with him or suffer the dislocation of his shoulder. He fell, and as he went down Glass drove both feet to his abdomen.

Broadbaker was shocked gasping, and now it was Glass' turn with the belt. He swung in a short, solid arc. The armed loops struck across Broadbaker's forehead. The strap end of the belt wrapped itself around his head, and when Glass reared back, it nearly tore his head from his spine.

The advantage his, Glass would gladly have stepped free. He wanted room for a full swing. But their hands were locked. Broadbaker, doubling his left arm, pulled himself to a sitting position and, with his greater weight, jerked Glass to the earth in front of him. Braced boot to boot, they traded blows. The heavily weighted belts left neither with much capability for thought. Slugged to semiconsciousness, they acted through savage instinct. They moved like animals from the primeval darkness, locked in a duel from which there was no retreat. Slowly brutally, methodically they beat each other into insensibility. The pace had slowed. Neither man had the reflexes to so much as turn his head or lift a shoulder to break the blows. It was as if each deliberately offered himself as a challenge for the worst his adversary could offer. They would take the impact. There would be a moment of rising from it, a gathering of strength. Then with a lift and grunt each would smash the armed and weighted belt to the side of his adversary's head. The belts struck with a heavy sound repeatedly, regularly, and it seemed for a while that both men would sink to oblivion, bleeding and broken, and that there would be nothing left but bloody stumps where their heads had been.

But slowly, steadily, the tide turned to Broadbaker. His belt was more heavily weighted with cartridges, a disadvantage in the quick maneuvering but an advantage now. Every blow was heavier. And it was backed by the twenty or thirty extra pounds of muscle and bone. Now each time Glass hit him, he took it stolidly, apparently unblinking, but his return, up and over with shocking force, made Glass crumple a little. The sides of their heads were beaten out of shape, cut and bleeding, with battered skin mixing with hair. One of Broadbaker's ears had been torn by a downward blow, so that it hung by half its skin and cartilage. It ran blood in a swift stream, and each time he swung, the ear flopped and sprayed blood across Glass' face. Broadbaker knew he was winning. He sensed victory in his bones, in his deep fibers, and his spirits rose. Now each time he swung, he shouted, and it was like a laugh. He got slowly to his feet with Glass hanging to him. He was ready to finish the contest. One more, or one more, or surely the one after that would leave Glass hanging unconscious, and then slowly, taking his time, he could beat the head to splintered bones. There was no mercy in him. No beholder doubted that Broadbaker intended to kill him.

"Stop it! Why doesn't somebody stop it?" Polly Arbogast was saying, trying to get over and grab the belt. But men held her. When at last she got through them and grabbed Broadbaker's arm, he ripped free, knocking her spinning to hands and knees and probably not even knowing he had done so.

Glass managed to rise halfway to his feet. When Broadbaker set his boots for the final, terrible blow, he dived forward. He struck shoulders against Broadbaker's knees. Somehow he summoned the power to carry the big man backward. They went into the brush and fought through it crashing. They staggered and climbed a low brushy bank and fell and rolled and got up again, hands still locked so neither could free himself, so neither could have released his hold if he had willed it, a living death grip.

Broadbaker, with certain victory ripped from him, was cursing in a hoarse voice. He kept trying to set himself for another swing of the belt, but he found the footing soft, the brush at angle that clung to his clothes, and each time he tried to bring the belt around, it struck something, making it lose direction and force of impact.

And so they came to a ten-foot bank overhanging a dry channel of the river. Below, like the bones of some prehistoric monster, white in the moonlight, lay a cast-up drift of cottonwood trunks. Sand had settled among them and there were a few green things growing. The stubbed, broken limbs of the trees stuck out a foot or two like blunt spears. In daylight, with care, a man could have crossed, but at night they constituted a trap and one of the valley's worst dangers to blundering horsemen.

At a running, belt-wielding series of pivots the two men reached this edge. A mass of dirt fell, but Glass, with his back to the drop-off, saved himself. He lunged and came up bearing Broadbaker on his shoulders.

Broadbaker lashed at him, but his feet had been ripped from the ground. He saw the abyss with its log tangle and with a cry attempted to free himself. He went head down and over, carrying Glass with him. He struck flat on his back with a crash of shattered wood. His weight, coming with pounding force, cracked one of the logs. But a stubbed branch stood upright. It impaled him like a blunt javelin. He struck it squarely, and its jagged end passed through his chest, breaking his ribs back and front and thrusting up his shirt like a bloody tent pole. His breath came in an exhaling scream. With head back, lips peeled over his teeth, and eyes staring out of his skull, he writhed trying to free himself of the terrible impalement. From some reserve of energy he managed a final effort. He kicked, treading his body in a quarter-circle around the branch. He even managed to get his legs doubled under him and form a bridge, lifting his hips and the small of his back.

Then with a groan the breath and the muscle tension left him. He went limp, and his feet hung, his head hung, and the log turned a little with his weight, and he was still.

Glass, although dragged by Broadbaker in the fall, saved himself by falling atop him and by dropping the gun belt and seizing an overhanging chokecherry branch, which broke his descent. He stood among the logs with his boots in rotting wood and sand. Now he tried to remove his hand, but Broadbaker held him in the clamp of a death grip. His tendons might have been steel cable. His muscles were hard as granite. Glass hunted his pockets for something to pry with, but all he could find was a silver dollar. Men came around from both sides, trying to see.

"He's dead," a man said. "That branch thick as your arm punched right through him."

"Who? Who?" the girl was crying.

"Broadbaker, that's who," said Old Dad, awed and grateful. "He finally got his. By God, he got his!"

They pried Broadbaker's fingers loose with a bowie knife. The logs were pulled away so Glass could walk out. He had no memory of doing it. His feet moved by themselves, for a long time he had no use of his hand. By using his right hand to open and close the fingers he finally brought action and feeling back to it. They had a lantern — a candle and tin-can affair — and were looking at Broadbaker. He could hear them arguing about whether to pull him loose of the branch or get an axe and chop the log from under him. He turned his back. He did not want to look at him again, ever.

"We could just cave the bank over him and leave him here," a man said. And, "Well, anyhow, we'll know where to find him if we ever want him."

It won a burst of laughter. The laughter seemed ghoulish. He walked through the bushes. They ripped his beaten face. It was then he noticed how his face, neck, and left shoulder had been torn. Blood from somewhere — it proved to be a torn lower lip — kept running and dripping from his chin.

Polly had hold of him. He did not know how long she had been there. She led him, and he kept walking. The moon had begun to fade. It rode high and small in the sky. It was later than he imagined. It was past midnight. Some of the men were hunting dry wood to build a fire. They were soaked and cold and no Broadbaker now to tell them to drive the cattle in.

"Where's Lon?" he asked.

"I don't know. I'm going to look for him."

"Yes. Bring a horse. Where's my horse? Can I borrow a horse?"

"Use Broadbaker's," said a cowboy.

"No, I won't use Broadbaker's."

"Then, use Moffitt's," said Dad. "You want to know who got Moffitt? I got him. I put a .44 slug right through Moffitt!"

She led him to the fire, which had been built of dry wood from under a bank. A pitchlike substance boiled from it and it smelled like camphor.

"We need some clean water for your face," she said.

"Is it bad?" It felt thick and dead. He could talk from only one side of his mouth. When he closed his jaw, all his teeth seemed to have been knocked around wrong. He could turn only in one direction and then only a few degrees, and when he wanted to look around, it was necessary to turn his whole body. He had taken a fearful beating, but he was alive. He was alive and he felt that if he could just lie full length, perfectly still, just lie there for a little while . . .

"The river water is all right," Old Dad was saying. "You know what's really best for that? Plain old gumbo mud. Yes, sir, you take cool gumbo mud and spread it real thick under a wet sack it will absorb swelling, pain, everything. It's a real poultice. I had a dog once, a blue-tick hound, and he was clawed by a mountain lion until his skin was hanging on him like rags, and all swollen and maggoty, and by the gods he went and buried himself in the mud so only his nose was sticking out, and in three or four days . . . "

"Just bury me in the mud," said Glass, and tried to laugh. He lay down and let her do with him as she wanted. It made him feel very good, despite pain and dizziness and the leaden fatigue, to know she was with him.

A great many things happened. He knew when it was daylight and when the sun was hot through canvas. Somehow he had been placed in a wagon without his knowing it, and now the wagon, was moving along. It rocked steadily over uneven ground. He was in no pain. Only when he moved or tried to sit up. When he lay perfectly still, when he relaxed in every fiber, then the movement became almost pleasant. He got so he could anticipate each of the major bumps, first the front wheel and next the rear. Then for a while there were no bumps at all, only an easy, padded rocking. They were crossing a lake bed. The mud had dried in cracked, square saucers, and he could hear them crunch as the wheels passed over them.

There was a man in the wagon with him. He got it into his head that the man was Maybee. Good old Kid Maybee! The man who gave him the chance to make $10,000, $9,000 at the very least, driving cattle to the Montana gold camps.

"I'm all cured," said Will.

"Hello, Kid," he said.

A strange voice answered him, but he couldn't get it out of his head that Kid Maybee was there.

"I always heard bad things about you, Kid. You sent me into a wa-hoo with the Man-Eater and no warning. You sent me in here to save a herd you'd never be able to save yourself. I should cut you off without a cent. But I won't. A deal's a deal."

By jolting degrees, he woke up. He

was able to focus his eyes. The man wasn't Kid Maybee. The man was Lon Arbogast. "I thought you were dead," he said.

"No, I'm alive."

"You looked dead hanging onto the wagon. I figured the cattle had tromped you."

"No, they didn't come close. I just got a broken arm."

"Yes, I see. It's in the splints."

"I can wiggle my fingers." He showed him.

"Say, that's right!"

"Who'd you think I was? Kid who?"

"Kid Maybee. My half-and-half partner."

"I thought Dad was your half-and-half partner."

"He is. I'm divided up for fair. I'll be lucky to have wages left. I got that German kid to think about, too."

"Otto?"

"Otto Hoess. I sort of promised to set him up in the steam engine business. This wagon is jolting so much I can't exactly recall what I did promise. Who's driving this wagon?"

"Young Pattison."

"He shouldn't be. He'll open his wound again."

"No, he's all right."

"I owe him ten dollars a month and found. Then there's his folks. I got to check and see about Mrs. Pattison's gallstones. I can't just abandon 'em in Casper. I got to get in there and see if they can travel. If they can't wagon-travel, I'll have to see they get coach passage over to Soda Springs and then up to Montana by the Beaverhead road. That'll cost a pretty penny. I'm not my own man at all. I don't have to be responsible for Broadbaker's cattle, do I?"

"No, I'll take over. He had people in Texas. We'll have to turn his estate over to the court."

"The first worry is finding a range for those cattle." He tried to get to his feet. "Stop the wagon!"

Young Pattison drew up and watched

through the front opening while Glass got to his feet.

"Wasn't it your plan to winter on the Popo?"

Polly rode up in time to hear him. "No, we're not going to the Popo! How do you feel?"

"I don't know. I guess I feel pretty good."

Yes, he did. In spite of the bruises and swellings and the teeth that didn't fit together quite right, he felt very good. Outside, he noticed, the prairie looked very bright and fresh. It was the rain. Everything smelled like spring.

"In fact, I think I'll drive for a while."

"You can sit up front while I do the driving."

"Can I ride your bronc, Miss Polly?" asked Will.

Glass said, "Stay off that bronc. You'll bust your wound open. You and Lonnie can have a turn at my bed."

"Yes, you can ride the bronc," said Polly.

Glass didn't argue. He got into the seat. They were traveling across a shelf of prairie miles wide with the valley of a river far ahead of them. Other wagons could be seen in the distance, and the cattle, moving peacefully after their run of the night before.

"Where we headed?" he asked. "I got to meet Parsons at Teakettle Rock."

"I know," she said. "That's where I'm headed. That's where we're all headed."

"You two goin' to get married?" asked young Will, who was staying close and listening to every word.

"Of course we are!" said Polly.

Glass heard her with wonder but didn't say a word.

"I was just curious," said Will. "That don't interfere with me gettin' to be foreman, does it, Mr. Glass?"

"Foreman is a job you got to grow into, son."

"I know, but I still got the inside track, haven't I?"

He rode beside them waiting for an

answer, but he noticed that Glass had his eyes closed and his head on the girl's shoulder.

"Foreman for Glass and Arbogast! That'll be a *big* job. *Mighty* big!"

THE END

FIGHTING RAMROD
Charles N. Heckelmann

Most men would have cut their losses, but Frazer counted the bullets in his guns and said he'd soak the range in blood before he'd give up another inch of what was his.

LONE GUN
Eric Allen

Smoke Blackbird had been away too long. The Lequires had seized the Blackbird farm, forcing the Indians and settlers off, and no one seemed willing to fight! He had to fight alone.

THE THIRD RIDER
Barry Cord

Mel Rawlins wasn't going to let anything stand in his way. His father was murdered, his two brothers gone. Now Mel rode for vengeance.

ARIZONA DRIFTERS
W. C. Tuttle

When drifting Dutton and Lonnie Steelman decide to become partners they find that they have a common enemy in the formidable Thurston brothers.

TOMBSTONE
Matt Braun

Wells Fargo paid Luke Starbuck to outgun the silver-thieving stagecoach gang at Tombstone. Before long Luke can see the only thing bearing fruit in this eldorado will be the gallows tree.

HIGH BORDER RIDERS
Lee Floren

Buckshot McKee and Tortilla Joe cut the trail of a border tough who was running Mexican beef into Texas. They stopped the smuggler in his tracks.

BRETT RANDALL, GAMBLER
E. B. Mann

Larry Day had the choice of running away from the law or of assuming a dead man's place. No matter what he decided he was bound to end up dead.

THE GUNSHARP
William R. Cox

The Eggerleys weren't very smart. They trained their sights on Will Carney and Arizona's biggest blood bath began.

THE DEPUTY OF SAN RIANO
Lawrence A. Keating and
Al. P. Nelson

When a man fell dead from his horse, Ed Grant was spotted riding away from the scene. The deputy sheriff rode out after him and came up against everything from gunfire to dynamite.

FARGO: MASSACRE RIVER
John Benteen

The ambushers up ahead had now blocked the road. Fargo's convoy was a jumble, a perfect target for the insurgents' weapons!

SUNDANCE: DEATH IN THE LAVA
John Benteen

The Modoc's captured the wagon train and its cargo of gold. But now the halfbreed they called Sundance was going after it . . .

HARSH RECKONING
Phil Ketchum

Five years of keeping himself alive in a brutal prison had made Brand tough and careless about who he gunned down . . .

FARGO: PANAMA GOLD
John Benteen

With foreign money behind him, Buckner was going to destroy the Panama Canal before it could be completed. Fargo's job was to stop Buckner.

FARGO:
THE SHARPSHOOTERS
John Benteen

The Canfield clan, thirty strong were raising hell in Texas. Fargo was tough enough to hold his own against the whole clan.

PISTOL LAW
Paul Evan Lehman

Lance Jones came back to Mustang for just one thing — revenge! Revenge on the people who had him thrown in jail.

HELL RIDERS
Steve Mensing

Wade Walker's kid brother, Duane, was locked up in the Silver City jail facing a rope at dawn. Wade was a ruthless outlaw, but he was smart, and he had vowed to have his brother out of jail before morning!

DESERT OF THE DAMNED
Nelson Nye

The law was after him for the murder of a marshal — a murder he didn't commit. Breen was after him for revenge — and Breen wouldn't stop at anything . . . blackmail, a frameup . . . or murder.

DAY OF THE COMANCHEROS
Steven C. Lawrence

Their very name struck terror into men's hearts — the Comancheros, a savage army of cutthroats who swept across Texas, leaving behind a bloodstained trail of robbery and murder.

SUNDANCE: SILENT ENEMY
John Benteen

A lone crazed Cheyenne was on a personal war path. They needed to pit one man against one crazed Indian. That man was Sundance.

LASSITER
Jack Slade

Lassiter wasn't the kind of man to listen to reason. Cross him once and he'll hold a grudge for years to come — if he let you live that long.

LAST STAGE TO GOMORRAH
Barry Cord

Jeff Carter, tough ex-riverboat gambler, now had himself a horse ranch that kept him free from gunfights and card games. Until Sturvesant of Wells Fargo showed up.

McALLISTER
ON THE
COMANCHE CROSSING
Matt Chisholm

The Comanche, McAllister owes them a life — and the trail is soaked with the blood of the men who had tried to outrun them before.

QUICK-TRIGGER COUNTRY
Clem Colt

Turkey Red hooked up with Curly Bill Graham's outlaw crew. But wholesale murder was out of Turk's line, so when range war flared he bucked the whole border gang alone . . .

CAMPAIGNING
Jim Miller

Ambushed on the Santa Fe trail, Sean Callahan is saved by two Indian strangers. But there'll be more lead and arrows flying before the band join Kit Carson against the Comanches.

GUNSLINGER'S RANGE
Jackson Cole

Three escaped convicts are out for revenge. They won't rest until they put a bullet through the head of the dirty snake who locked them behind bars.

RUSTLER'S TRAIL
Lee Floren

Jim Carlin knew he would have to stand up and fight because he had staked his claim right in the middle of Big Ike Outland's best grass.

THE TRUTH ABOUT SNAKE RIDGE
Marshall Grover

The troubleshooters came to San Cristobal to help the needy. For Larry and Stretch the turmoil began with a brawl and then an ambush.

WOLF DOG RANGE
Lee Floren

Will Ardery would stop at nothing, unless something stopped him first — like a bullet from Pete Manly's gun.

DEVIL'S DINERO
Marshall Grover

Plagued by remorse, a rich old reprobate hired the Texas Troubleshooters to deliver a fortune in greenbacks to each of his victims.

GUNS OF FURY
Ernest Haycox

Dane Starr, alias Dan Smith, wanted to close the door on his past and hang up his guns, but people wouldn't let him.

DONOVAN
Elmer Kelton

Donovan was supposed to be dead. Uncle Joe Vickers had fired off both barrels of a shotgun into the vicious outlaw's face as he was escaping from jail. Now Uncle Joe had been shot — in just the same way.

CODE OF THE GUN
Gordon D. Shirreffs

MacLean came riding home, with saddle tramp written all over him, but sewn in his shirt-lining was an Arizona Ranger's star.

GAMBLER'S GUN LUCK
Brett Austen

Gamblers seldom live long. Parker was a hell of a gambler. It was his life — or his death . . .

DAY OF THE BUZZARD
T. V. Olsen

All Val Penmark cared about was getting the men who killed his wife.

THE MANHUNTER
Gordon D. Shirreffs

Lee Kershaw knew that every Rurale in the territory was on the lookout for him. But the offer of $5,000 in gold to find five small pieces of leather was too good to turn down.